The Time Traveller Book of KNIGHTS and CASTLES

Judy Hindley

Illustrated by Toni Goffe
Designed by John Jamieson

Contents

2　The People You Will Meet in This Book

3　Going Back in Time

4　Journey to a Castle

6　Beyond the Castle Walls

8　Inside the Keep

10　Dawn at the Castle

12　Going Hunting

14　Having a Feast

16　Trip to a Building Site

18　Trip to Town

20　The Training of a Knight

22　A Squire Becomes a Knight

24　At the Scene of a Joust

26　Return From the Crusades

28　The Castle is Attacked

30　Castle Map

32　Index
　　Going Further

First published in 1976
by Usborne Publishing Ltd
Usborne House, 83-85 Saffron Hill
London EC1N 8RT, England

Copyright © 1993, 1976 Usborne Publishing Ltd.

Printed in Belgium UE

The People You Will Meet in This Book

Everyone you will meet in this book has special duties and work to do. People are born with these duties, and have little chance to change their way of life.

This is mainly because life for these people is hard and dangerous—like life on a ship or in an army. The comfort and safety of each person depends on the work of all the others.

For example, there must be strong leaders, like Baron Godfrey, to protect people from enemies and criminals. But the baron needs his people, too—to work and fight for him.

Everyone must obey God and the king. God is obeyed through his Church, which has its own leaders. The Church's ruler is the Pope.

SIMON, KNIGHT

TROUBADOUR

A knight is a fighting man with special privileges. You can become a knight by training as a squire or by showing great skill and bravery in battle. Some knights are also poets and musicians, like the travelling minstrels. These knights are called troubadours.

ROBERT, SQUIRE

A squire must be of noble birth—the son of another knight, or someone with a title, such as baron. He is a trainee-knight.

MAN-AT-ARMS

A man-at-arms has the arms and equipment of a knight, but not the title of knight.

FOOT SOLDIER

A foot-soldier is a fighting man who is not of noble birth. Knights always fight on horseback.

2

BARON GODFREY

LADY ALICE

Baron Godfrey is a knight and a nobleman. He owns land. His job is to protect his land and people, and to see that his people live peacefully together, keeping the laws. He is the lord of many less powerful knights.

BISHOP

PRIEST

A priest is the religious leader of the people in his parish. His lord is the bishop, who has many parishes and a great church called a cathedral.

FRIAR

A friar is a priest without a parish. Friars travel about, trying to serve God by teaching and preaching.

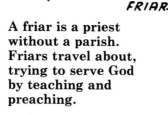

NUN

MONK

Monks and nuns are people who have promised to serve God by work and prayer, and sometimes by teaching and helping people.

LADY ANNA

Each lady must obey her husband, or her father if she is not married, as well as her king.

Many noble ladies live in the castle. Lady Alice gives them a home and helps teach the young girls. In return they help and obey her.

STEWARD

A steward is a head servant. Some can read and write a bit, and do large sums. Few other people can.

SERVANT →

Servants must obey the people they work for. They live in the houses or castles of their masters.

PEASANT

Peasants belong to the land of a certain lord. They may not leave it. The lord may let them farm some of it for themselves, in return for the work they do for him.

 SERFS →

Serfs are slaves. Many are the children of foreigners who were captured in wars and sold to the rich.

Going Back in Time

The people you have just met are not real people – at least, as far as we know. But all the things they do are things real people have done. All over Europe you can see the castles they lived in. In museums you can find some of the actual furniture they used, and pictures of people taking baths and playing with pets just like the people in this book.

But museums cannot often show everything you want to see, all in one place. And real castles are often half-destroyed, and empty. You may often have wished you could go back in time to see how a castle looked when the fire was roaring on the hearth, and the tapestries were bright, and people were talking and laughing in the candle-light.

We have invented a magic time helmet to help you make this trip. Below you can see how it works.

Put on the Helmet

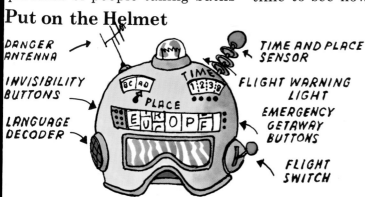

Here is the magic Time helmet. You can set the 'Place' and 'Time' dials to go back in time to any place you like. There are lots of gadgets for emergencies. All you have to do is pick your destination.

Pick Your Destination

We know there were lots of castles in north-west Europe in about 1240. And we know this was a great time for knightly deeds and adventures. So let us set the 'Place' dial for this bit—and let us start going back.

Our first stop is in 1940, before your mum and dad were born. Notice the big, funny-looking radio.

Now we have gone back another forty years. Perhaps your great-great-grandfather is a baby now. A lot of things are different.

Now we have jumped a century. Houses are heated by log fires and lit by candles, and many families go to bed early to save fuel.

We have really come a long way, now. Even books are a luxury. We are almost on the last lap of our journey—turn the page, and see.

Journey to a Castle

You are in Europe in the year 1240. You find yourself in rough, dangerous country. Long ago, the Romans built roads and cities here. But most of the Romans left 600 years ago, and often their cities crumbled. The biggest buildings you see now are cathedrals, and the great castles built by the kings and fighting barons.

The countries of Europe are not like those you know. They have different names and languages. They hardly seem like countries—few have really strong kings and governments.

All over Europe, powerful barons are fighting each other for land. Each tries to gather as many knights as he can, and build the strongest castle. He rules over all his land.

The peasants in this village cannot leave Baron Godfrey's land—unless they grow rich enough to buy their freedom, or brave enough to escape to a big town.

Animals and people still do many kinds of hard work—like this farmer and his oxen.

This is one of the first kinds of machine. The stream turns the wheel and the axle of the wheel turns a stone inside the hut. The heavy stone grinds wheat into flour.

WATERMILL

AXLE

Over the last two centuries, many thousands of watermills have been built. They do lots of work that used to be done by serfs. The whole country is a little bit richer now.

Baron Godfrey owns several castles, miles apart. He and his family, knights and servants eat the food grown on the castle lands. When it runs out, they move on.

TAPESTRIES

BARON GODFREY

BEST CANDLESTICKS

Baron Godfrey takes everything valuable with him, in case his castle is conquered while he is gone. He takes food for the journey too. The carts only travel about 30 km a day.

How We Know What a Time

We have lots of clues to help u work out how people lived in t past. We can still see many of their writings, buildings and tools—and pictures they paint like those above.

4

All the land in this picture belongs to the Baron. The people who live here must work for him and obey his laws. With his knights and men-at-arms, he protects them from enemies and criminals.

BARON GODFREY'S CASTLE

This winding track was here before Roman times. Roman roads run straight over the hills and across the fields.

ROMAN ROAD

You must take a ferry to cross this river. Bridges are not reliable. You often find they have been burned or destroyed in some battle between barons.

FERRY

Half the countryside is forest. It is full of wild animals—deer, bears, wild boars and fierce grey wolves. In a hard winter, hungry wolves from the forest may kill the villagers' pigs and chickens.

Letters are carried by hand. All news must come by messenger or from a traveller of some kind. People are always looking out for a bit of news.

MESSENGER

WILD BOARS

The big game in the forest, like deer and bears, belongs to the Baron. But peasants hunt for small game, and scavenge for nuts, mushrooms and firewood.

MINSTRELS

Minstrels live by entertaining people with songs and stories and the latest news. They wander from place to place—everyone welcomes them.

PEASANTS

Traveller Would Find

However, there are still many mysteries and missing clues. Historians are people who work at solving these mysteries. We had to ask several historians for help with this book.

History is like a detective story that never really ends. New clues are always being discovered, and new ideas about what the clues might mean.

Perhaps you, one day, will find a new clue, or a new solution to one of the puzzles of history. 'Going Further', on page 32, tells more about what to read and what to look for.

Beyond the Castle Walls

Baron Godfrey's castle is very strong. It is almost impossible for an enemy to get in. Behind the wall at the back is a steep cliff. Round the front and sides are a deep ditch and two rows of heavily defended walls. The entrance is like an obstacle course—the pictures below show how difficult it is to get through it.

What you find beyond the gates is almost a little town. The castle has its own carpenters and its own thatchers and masons to keep the thatched roofs and stone walls repaired. It has shoemakers and blacksmiths, tailors and armourers. There are stables, water, food supplies—even a

fishpond. If you were besieged, you might live here quite comfortably for weeks.

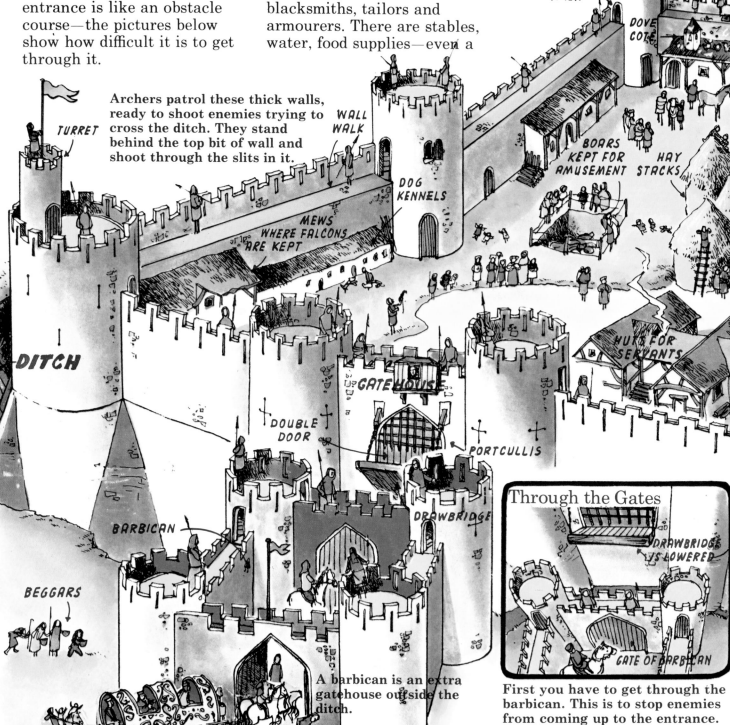

Archers patrol these thick walls, ready to shoot enemies trying to cross the ditch. They stand behind the top bit of wall and shoot through the slits in it.

TURRET

WALL WALK

DOOR TO WALL WALK

DOVE COTE

DOG KENNELS

BOARS KEPT FOR AMUSEMENT

HAY STACKS

MEWS WHERE FALCONS ARE KEPT

HUTS FOR SERVANTS

DITCH

GATEHOUSE

DOUBLE DOOR

PORTCULLIS

BARBICAN

DRAWBRIDGE

BEGGARS

A barbican is an extra gatehouse outside the ditch.

Through the Gates

DRAWBRIDGE IS LOWERED

GATE OF BARBICAN

First you have to get through the barbican. This is to stop enemies from coming up to the entrance. (They might fill up the ditch.)

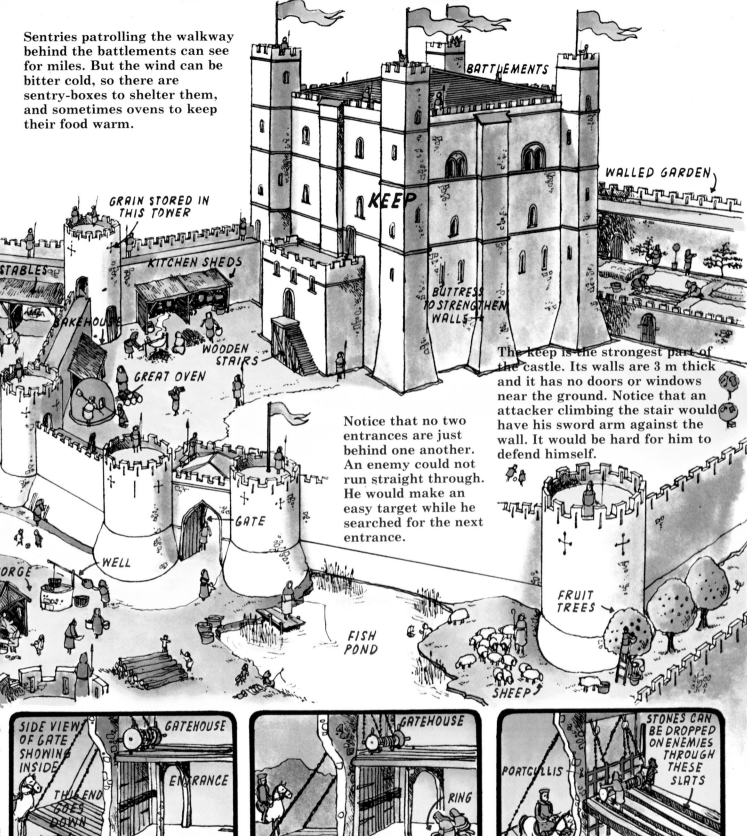

Sentries patrolling the walkway behind the battlements can see for miles. But the wind can be bitter cold, so there are sentry-boxes to shelter them, and sometimes ovens to keep their food warm.

BATTLEMENTS

WALLED GARDEN

KEEP

GRAIN STORED IN THIS TOWER

KITCHEN SHEDS

STABLES

BAKEHOUSE

WOODEN STAIRS

GREAT OVEN

BUTTRESS TO STRENGTHEN WALLS

The keep is the strongest part of the castle. Its walls are 3 m thick and it has no doors or windows near the ground. Notice that an attacker climbing the stair would have his sword arm against the wall. It would be hard for him to defend himself.

Notice that no two entrances are just behind one another. An enemy could not run straight through. He would make an easy target while he searched for the next entrance.

GATE

FORGE

WELL

FISH POND

FRUIT TREES

SHEEP

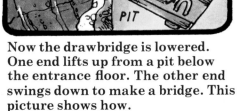

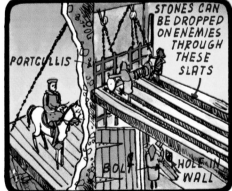

SIDE VIEW OF GATE SHOWING INSIDE

GATEHOUSE

ENTRANCE

THIS END GOES DOWN

THIS GOES UP

PIT

GATEHOUSE

RING

PIT

BOLT

PORTCULLIS

STONES CAN BE DROPPED ON ENEMIES THROUGH THESE SLATS

BOLT

HOLE IN WALL

Now the drawbridge is lowered. One end lifts up from a pit below the entrance floor. The other end swings down to make a bridge. This picture shows how.

Now the drawbridge is bolted into place. The entrance is still defended by an iron grill called a portcullis, and big double doors.

Now the portcullis is raised. It slides up grooves in the walls. The doors are unbolted. You can see these grooves and bolt-holes in many castles.

Inside the Keep

The keep is where the baron's family lives, together with knights, men-at-arms, servants and friends.

This keep was built two hundred years ago—about 1040. Then it was a draughty, cold and gloomy place. Many young squires died coughing. But now it is much more comfortable and cheerful. The walls are hung with rugs from crusader lands, there is glass in some of the windows, and the fireplaces give more heat and less smoke.

The courtyard round the keep is thronged with travellers—pilgrims, pedlars, traders, and the barefoot friars who wander Europe teaching and preaching.

In the upper rooms of the keep women sew, weave and embroider, listening to the songs and poems of troubadours. Sometimes the friars read to them and even bring them the latest teachings on philosophy and science. A few of these women are among the best-educated people in Europe. Some become troubadours themselves, like the famous Marie de France.

Lots of Lady Alice's friends live in the castle—aunts, cousins and other noble ladies. They make clothes and cushions and tapestries

THIS LADY IS WEAVING A TAPESTRY

Notice the direction in which stair curves. This helps people defend the tower. An attacker climbing up would find it very hard to use his sword.

"Peace, oh my stricken lute"

TROUBADOUR

BARON

DUNGEON

KITCHEN SHEDS

THATCHER REPAIRING ROOF

One of the steward's jobs is to settle quarrels and punish criminals. Baron Godfrey's stewards and bailiffs are his police.

SALT MERCHANT

STEWARD

HE STOLE MY PIG.

IT'S MY PIG!

Meat can be kept through the winter if it is salted or pickled with spices. You can get salt from sea-water, but many spices come only from certain countries. They are so important people fight wars about them.

PILGRIM

FRIAR

8

Maids look after Lady Alice's babies and children while Lady Alice looks after the rest of the castle people.

In her garden, Lady Alice has mint, thyme, fennel, parsley, sage and hyssop to use for cooking and medicine. But she says, 'The best doctors are Dr. Quiet, Dr. Merry and Dr. Diet.'

People believe that some herbs should be planted, gathered and swallowed under certain stars. If parsley is planted on Good Friday, it is supposed to cure sick fish.

MAIDS

BARON'S BEDROOM

CHAPLAIN

CHAPEL

GARDEROBE

Tiny rooms and cupboards and passages are cut into these thick outer walls. The garderobe is a lavatory. It has no plumbing—just a hole going down through the wall.

GREAT HALL

BEAMS

These fireplaces have short chimneys which go through the wall instead of up to the roof. They can make the rooms very smoky if the wind blows from the wrong direction.

VAULTED BASEMENT

STOREROOM

Pork, timber, game, corn, bacon, cheese and many other supplies come from the lord's own land.

Stocks of food are kept here for emergencies. Precious things like spices and sugar are stored here, too. It is a bit like a shop. Records are kept of whatever goes in or out.

WHAT'S THE NEWS?

The castle people make their own soap. They save up the laundry and do a lot at once, boiling it in cauldrons and hanging it to dry like this.

9

Dawn at the Castle

Your first night in the castle has ended. At dawn the great bell is rung. Everyone wakes.

The air is so cold that many people wear night-caps to keep their heads warm.

At night, with the windows shuttered, the castle is dark as a cave. A huge candle burns all night in the baron's room.

The baron's bed is a wooden frame filled with straw. The mattress sits on top. The curtains make it snug and private.

No one has a bedroom to himself. Several of the baron's servants sleep in the same room with him and his lady —as well as his dogs and children.

Most people sleep on pallets—mattresses stuffed with straw or feathers. At dawn these can be rolled up and tucked away.

Servants wake early to light the fires and bring breakfast. There is no tea or coffee, few people like milk, and plain water carries illnesses. So even children have beer with their bread.

Some of the men sleep in their cloaks round the warm embers of the hearth. When they wake, they are already dressed.

Rushes and straw make the floor feel warmer. They soak up spills from the table during the day. When they get dirty, they are just swept out.

10

Baron Godfrey Gets Dressed

BEFORE HE GETS UP HE PUTS ON HIS SHIRT.

HE SHAVES BY RUBBING HIS WHISKERS OFF WITH A ROUGH PUMICE STONE.

HE IS HELPED ON WITH HIS LONG HOSE.

HIS SHOES FASTEN UP WITH A BUTTON.

HIS ROBE IS LINED WITH FUR.

A USEFUL BAG SLIDES ONTO HIS BELT.

Lady Alice Gets Dressed

SHE WEARS A TUNIC

AND ROBE CALLED A SURCOAT.

HER HAIR IS BRAIDED

COILED ROUND HER EARS

COVERED WITH A BAND OF CLOTH

AND TOPPED OFF WITH A HAT.

And Others Get Dressed

MONKS AND NUNS SPEND THEIR LIVES HELPING PEOPLE AND SERVING GOD.

THEIR LONG ROBES SHOW THEY ARE SPECIAL.

GIRLS WEAR THEIR HAIR LOOSE, BUT DRESS JUST LIKE THEIR MOTHERS.

BOYS DRESS LIKE THEIR FATHERS—THEY EVEN CARRY DAGGERS IN THEIR BELTS.

WORKERS AND SERVANTS WEAR SENSIBLE, TOUGH CLOTHES.

ON WET DAYS, WORKING PEOPLE WEAR CLOGS TO KEEP THEIR FEET DRY.

Taking a Bath

IT TAKES A LONG TIME TO HEAT ENOUGH BUCKETS OF WATER TO FILL A BATH, BECAUSE OF THIS PEOPLE OFTEN SHARE A BATH.

Baths are mostly for fun—or before a feast. Servants bring in a wooden tub and fill it with hot water. Since the soap does not smell very nice, they sprinkle the water with herbs and flowers.

THE SOAP IS MADE OF MUTTON FAT, WOOD ASH AND SODA. IT IS SOFT AND SQUISHY.

FLOWERS
HERBS
BOWL OF SOAP
HANDLES FOR CARRYING
THE TUB HAS HANDLES SO IT CAN BE CARRIED ROUND. IT HAS TO BE FILLED AND EMPTIED BY BUCKETS AND BAILERS.
BELLOWS TO MAKE FIRE BURN

11

Going on a Hunt

Baron Godfrey spends much of his life making war on enemy barons. His knights and men-at-arms must be well trained and always ready for battle. The knights practise fighting by having jousts and tournaments, which you can read about on pages 24 and 25. In good weather they spend the rest of their time in the woods and fields, riding with hounds and hawks.

These pages show how their sporting animals are trained, and how they hunt. There are great arguments between huntsmen and falconers over whether hounds or hawks are the most brave and noble company. In the evenings, their stories are told round the fire after splendid feasts of wild boar and venison.

The peasants and country people do not share this sport. Their fields and crops may be ruined by the hunt. They may be forced to give refreshment to the hunters from their own small supplies of food. And they themselves are not allowed to touch Baron Godfrey's game. These pages show some of their story, too.

Hunting a Stag

Soon the hounds will pick up the scent of game. Then the chase will begin . . . and no one knows where it will lead.

The spring seems very lovely when you have been shut inside through the long winter months. People sing and make music as they ride.

"If you were April's lady And I were lord of May"

Ladies ride with the hunt, singing and gossiping, their falcons on their wrists.

PEASANTS

These peasants are terrified by the sound of the hunt. They are poaching— hunting the baron's game. If caught, they will be punished.

TRAINING A FALCON

This is how falcons used to be trained. Today, Falcons are protected birds. It is **against the law** to steal eggs or baby birds.

* STRICTLY FORBIDDEN TODAY

KEEP THE BIRD IN A SAFE QUIET PLACE AT FIRST. FEED IT BY HAND SO THAT IT GETS TO KNOW YOU. WEAR A SPECIAL TOUGH GLOVE, SO IT CAN PERCH ON YOUR WRIST.

HOOD

BELL

WHEN THE BIRD IS TAME, PUT A LITTLE BELL ON ITS FOOT, AND LEASH IT. USE A HOOD TO KEEP IT CALM AND QUIET. THEN YOU CAN TAKE IT OUT FOR THE FIRST TIME.

Hounds and Their Kennels

Every day the kennel is swept and sprinkled with fresh straw.

The keeper of the hounds is paid a half penny a day besides his food and lodging. It is a good job, although he will have to save for eight days to buy a fur hat.

The hounds are treated much more gently than children. One of the stable boys sleeps in the kennel with them, to keep them calm during the night.

The huntsmen have chased for hours, through dense forest and brambles, and over ditches. They are tired, muddy and sore. But the horn leads them on.

This hunting horn is made from a stag's antler. It only plays one note. But the master of the hunt can signal by long and short blasts on it.

It has been a good hunt. The hounds were fast and fierce and cunning, and the stag ran hard. Music is played to honour the dying stag.

BEGIN BY LETTING THE FALCON FLY SHORT DISTANCES, ON ITS LEASH. WHISTLE IT BACK TO YOU—THEN REWARD IT WITH FOOD. BUT DO NOT OVERFEED IT.

WHEN IT IS FULLY TRAINED, TAKE IT OFF THE LEASH. IT WILL LEARN TO HUNT BY ITSELF. WATCH IT CAREFULLY. AFTER A WHILE YOU WILL SEE IT DIVE ON ITS PREY.

THE SOUND OF THE FALCON'S BELL WILL LEAD YOU TO IT THROUGH THE UNDERGROWTH. WHEN YOU TAKE IT AWAY FROM ITS PREY, ALWAYS REWARD YOUR BIRD WITH A BIT OF THE RAW MEAT.

Having a Feast

The 'kitchen' is just a group of sheds in the courtyard. Servants have been working here since dawn.

Spices and herbs must be ground up with a mortar and pestle. Lots of spices are used, to hide the taste of the meat. Without refrigerators, it goes bad quickly.

Much of the meat is roasted on spits in front of the fire. The servant boy who has to turn this spit is using an old, wet archery target as a fire screen.

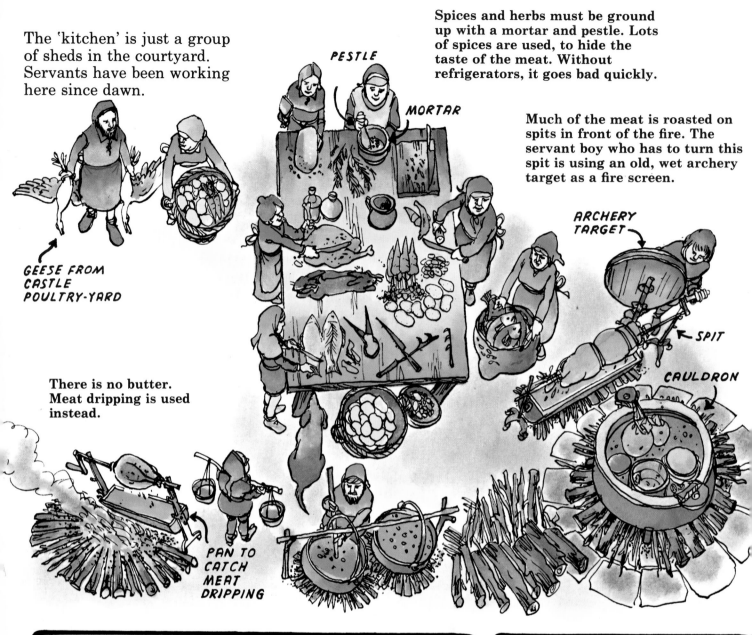

PESTLE

MORTAR

ARCHERY TARGET

SPIT

CAULDRON

GEESE FROM CASTLE POULTRY-YARD

There is no butter. Meat dripping is used instead.

PAN TO CATCH MEAT DRIPPING

Baking Bread

A fire is lit inside the oven to heat it while the dough is being made. Then the fire is raked out and the dough popped in, to bake as the oven cools.

Every bit of precious heat is used. After the bread is baked, the oven will be used for many other things, from making cakes to drying feathers and fuel.

Inside a Cauldron

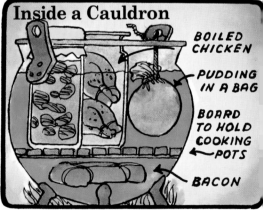

BOILED CHICKEN

PUDDING IN A BAG

BOARD TO HOLD COOKING POTS

BACON

Here are some of the things that might be cooked all together in a cauldron. Later the hot water will be used for washing up. Nothing will be wasted.

Sometimes food is scarce. In the winter, even rich people may live on beans and porridge. The poor often go hungry. During a famine some years ago they ate grass.

But at noon, in the great hall, the tables are always laid as well as possible. Baron Godfrey invites everyone— minstrels, traders, wandering knights. This is how he gets news of the world and keeps his friends. Everyone loves the music, games and stories.

It is late summer now, and the food is splendid. There will be four courses today, each with soup, fish, meat and sweets. Here are some of the dishes:

Boar's head with brawn pudding
Shellfish scented with jasmine,
　　rosemary and marigold
Fruit tarts
Salmon with orange
Beef with spices
Sugared nuts
Stuffed quarter of bear
Sugared mackerel
Squirrel stew
Apples and figs
Cakes with honey

Only the baron and Lady Alice (and perhaps some of their fine guests) have chairs. They sit at a special raised table— the 'high table'. The other tables are just boards resting on trestles.

Let no man laugh at us discomfited
But pray to God that He forgive us all

Eating a Meal

You must wash your hands before meals, since you eat with your fingers. Squires bring basins and pitchers to the fine people. The others use basins near the door.

Very few people use plates. One of the young squires serving at table will cut a slice of stale bread for you to put your food on. Later these will be given to the poor.

You use your own knife to cut up your meat. A platter of food is shared by two people, and usually you share a cup, too. You make friends quickly, this way.

15

Trip to a Building Site

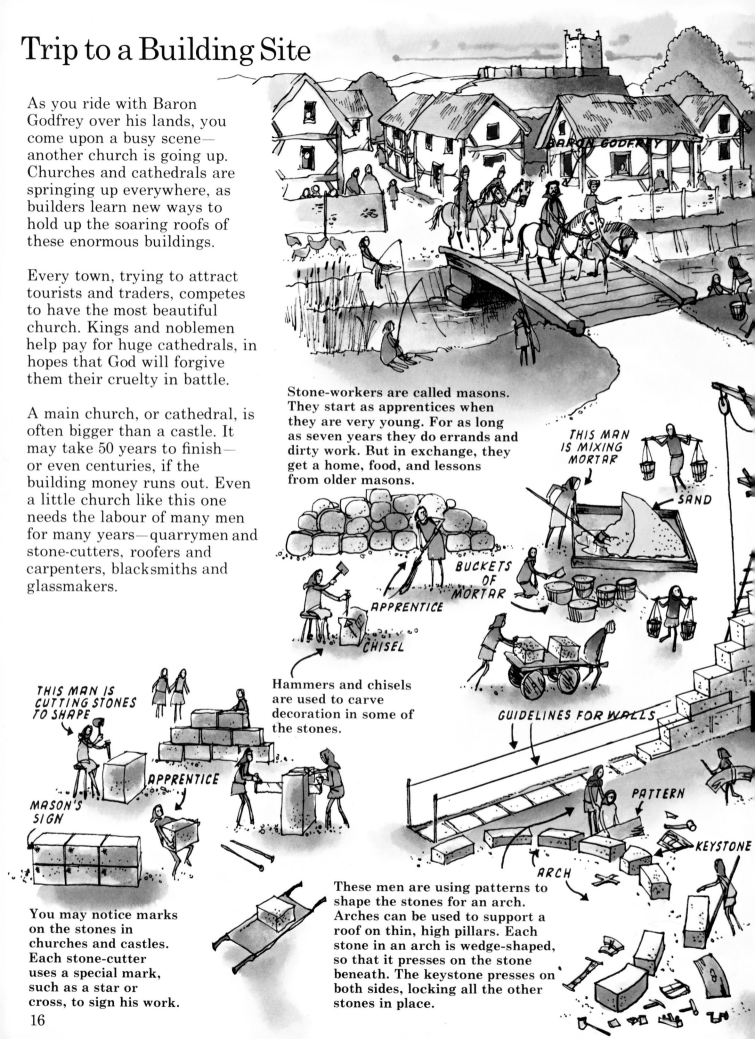

As you ride with Baron Godfrey over his lands, you come upon a busy scene—another church is going up. Churches and cathedrals are springing up everywhere, as builders learn new ways to hold up the soaring roofs of these enormous buildings.

Every town, trying to attract tourists and traders, competes to have the most beautiful church. Kings and noblemen help pay for huge cathedrals, in hopes that God will forgive them their cruelty in battle.

A main church, or cathedral, is often bigger than a castle. It may take 50 years to finish— or even centuries, if the building money runs out. Even a little church like this one needs the labour of many men for many years—quarrymen and stone-cutters, roofers and carpenters, blacksmiths and glassmakers.

BARON GODFREY

Stone-workers are called masons. They start as apprentices when they are very young. For as long as seven years they do errands and dirty work. But in exchange, they get a home, food, and lessons from older masons.

THIS MAN IS MIXING MORTAR

SAND

APPRENTICE

CHISEL

BUCKETS OF MORTAR

Hammers and chisels are used to carve decoration in some of the stones.

GUIDELINES FOR WALLS

THIS MAN IS CUTTING STONES TO SHAPE

APPRENTICE

MASON'S SIGN

PATTERN

KEYSTONE

ARCH

You may notice marks on the stones in churches and castles. Each stone-cutter uses a special mark, such as a star or cross, to sign his work.

These men are using patterns to shape the stones for an arch. Arches can be used to support a roof on thin, high pillars. Each stone in an arch is wedge-shaped, so that it presses on the stone beneath. The keystone presses on both sides, locking all the other stones in place.

16

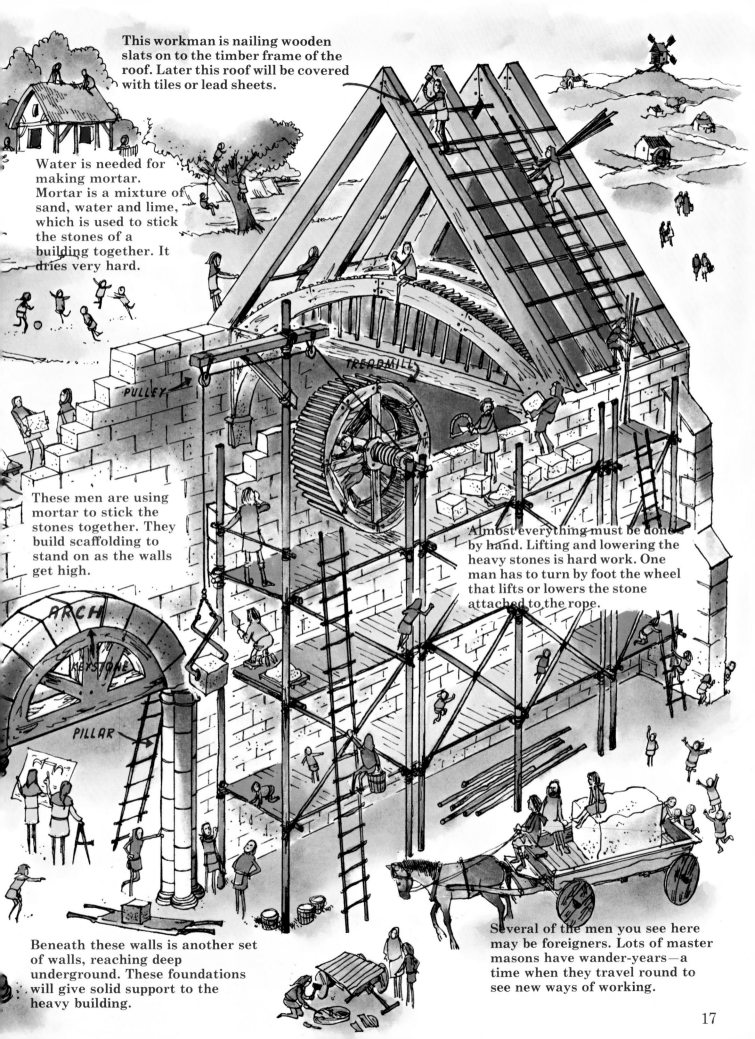

This workman is nailing wooden slats on to the timber frame of the roof. Later this roof will be covered with tiles or lead sheets.

Water is needed for making mortar. Mortar is a mixture of sand, water and lime, which is used to stick the stones of a building together. It dries very hard.

PULLEY

TREADMILL

These men are using mortar to stick the stones together. They build scaffolding to stand on as the walls get high.

ARCH

KEYSTONE

PILLAR

Almost everything must be done by hand. Lifting and lowering the heavy stones is hard work. One man has to turn by foot the wheel that lifts or lowers the stone attached to the rope.

Beneath these walls is another set of walls, reaching deep underground. These foundations will give solid support to the heavy building.

Several of the men you see here may be foreigners. Lots of master masons have wander-years—a time when they travel round to see new ways of working.

17

A Trip to Town

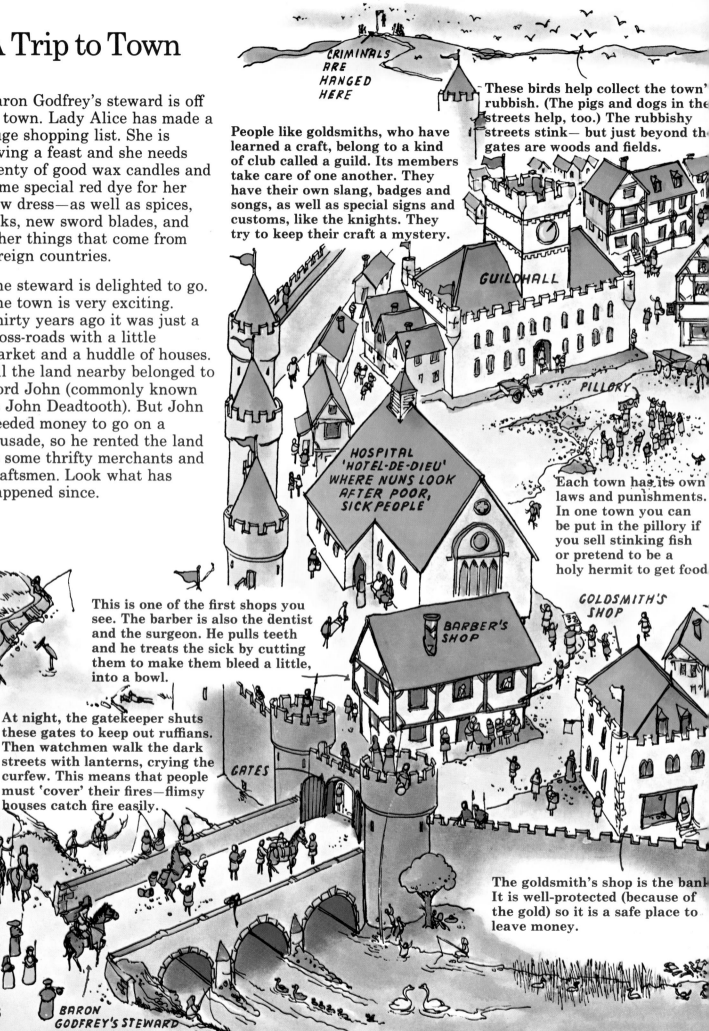

Baron Godfrey's steward is off to town. Lady Alice has made a huge shopping list. She is giving a feast and she needs plenty of good wax candles and some special red dye for her new dress—as well as spices, silks, new sword blades, and other things that come from foreign countries.

The steward is delighted to go. The town is very exciting. Thirty years ago it was just a cross-roads with a little market and a huddle of houses. All the land nearby belonged to Lord John (commonly known as John Deadtooth). But John needed money to go on a crusade, so he rented the land to some thrifty merchants and craftsmen. Look what has happened since.

CRIMINALS ARE HANGED HERE

People like goldsmiths, who have learned a craft, belong to a kind of club called a guild. Its members take care of one another. They have their own slang, badges and songs, as well as special signs and customs, like the knights. They try to keep their craft a mystery.

These birds help collect the town' rubbish. (The pigs and dogs in the streets help, too.) The rubbishy streets stink— but just beyond th gates are woods and fields.

GUILDHALL

PILLORY

HOSPITAL 'HOTEL-DE-DIEU' WHERE NUNS LOOK AFTER POOR, SICK PEOPLE

Each town has its own laws and punishments. In one town you can be put in the pillory if you sell stinking fish or pretend to be a holy hermit to get food

This is one of the first shops you see. The barber is also the dentist and the surgeon. He pulls teeth and he treats the sick by cutting them to make them bleed a little, into a bowl.

GOLDSMITH'S SHOP

BARBER'S SHOP

At night, the gatekeeper shuts these gates to keep out ruffians. Then watchmen walk the dark streets with lanterns, crying the curfew. This means that people must 'cover' their fires—flimsy houses catch fire easily.

GATES

The goldsmith's shop is the bank It is well-protected (because of the gold) so it is a safe place to leave money.

18

BARON GODFREY'S STEWARD

The church is always busy. Merchants meet here and sometimes bible plays are acted on the porch. People come to gossip as well as pray—and to see the story-pictures inside. A hunted criminal is safe from arrest if he stays near the altar.

OLD SQUIRE WOUNDED IN BATTLE

TOWN SQUARE

WATERING TROUGH

MARKET STALLS

RICH MEN HAVE THEIR OWN POLICE

This peasant is running away from Lord John. He hopes to become an apprentice and learn a trade. If he stays in the town for a year and a day he will be a free man.

ESCAPING PEASANT

Each market stall must buy a licence from the town council. This is one of the ways the council gets money. The council is a group of important townspeople who make laws and deal with things like fire protection.

PICKPOCKET AT WORK

This pilgrim is travelling to a saint's tomb. Then, he hopes, God will forgive his sins. You can tell he is a pilgrim by the cross he wears.

PILGRIM

TEACHER

PEOPLE ARE VERY FOND OF THEIR GARDENS

PILGRIM

The first universities started like this—just a few good teachers, selling knowledge. The lectures are in Latin, and people come to them from all over Europe.

Italian bankers are well-known for lending money as well as keeping it safe. They charge the borrower, and pay the lender for the use of the money. Of course, they take a bit extra for their trouble. The extra charges are called 'interest'.

MONEY LENDERS

Many Jews become money-lenders, because the Christian laws do not allow them to do much else. Some become very rich, which makes people jealous.

This river is the town's main water supply.

19

The Training of a Knight

You will notice lots of children round the castle. One of them is the baron's nephew, Robert. Like many boys of noble birth, Robert was sent to live with his uncle when he was very young—about six years old.

For many years, Robert served as a page, learning to be courteous and obedient. When he became a squire, at 14, he began training to be a knight.

His cousin, Simon, is about to take his knightly vows. Turn the page and see.

Learning About Armour

ROBERT

Robert helps his lord dress, and arms him for jousts and battles.

This teaches him how to use armour and look after it.

Archery Lessons

LOADING A CROSSBOW

Almost everyone learns to use a bow and arrow. Skilful hunters are always needed, particularly in winter, when food is scarce.

All the people in the castle love to hunt. But knights never use their cross-bows in a battle. They always fight man-to-man.

Riding Practice

Robert has to learn to ride one-handed, to keep his weapon arm free. He must train his horse to get used to noise—or it might bolt during a battle.

USING A LANCE

HE BRACES THE HEAVY LANCE AGAINST HIS SIDE TO STEADY IT. HE MUST AIM VERY CAREFULLY, OR THE LANCE WILL THROW HIM OFF-BALANCE WHEN IT STRIKES.

HERE THE YOUNG SQUIRE IS ABOUT TO GALLOP AT A SWIVELLING TARGET CALLED A QUINTAIN. HE HAS FIVE TRIES TO KNOCK IT DOWN BY HITTING IT DEAD CENTRE.

AT THE LAST MOMENT, HE RISES IN HIS STIRRUPS TO GET HIS WHOLE BODY BEHIND THE BLOW. IF THE BLOW IS OFF-CENTRE, THE TARGET SWINGS ROUND AND CLUBS HIM.

School

ABACUS (COUNTING STICKS)

He cleans rusty mail armour by rolling it in a barrel of sand.

The castle priest teaches Robert to read and write a little. Sometimes Lady Alice reads to him, and tells him stories of brave and famous people.

There is little paper, so he and his friends use pointed sticks and waxed tablets to practise writing. They need an abacus to do sums with Roman numerals.

Sword Practice

Games

Young boys use small, blunt swords or even wooden ones, and little round shields called bucklers. They slash with the sword's edge, catching blows with the sword or the buckler.

As the boys get stronger they use heavier weapons. The sharp-edged battle sword weighs about 1½kg. It can slice through armour, cutting off arms and legs.

While the knights practise jousting, the squires wrestle and fight and 'joust' with wooden sticks and horses.

When knights and older squires come round, the small boys must be ready for a rough time. No one is very gentle—a knight must learn to be tough.

A Squire Becomes a Knight

The time has come for Simon to be dubbed a knight. Several of his friends will be knighted with him. Tomorrow, after the ceremony, there will be feasts and jousts and gifts from the new knights to their friends.

But first, they spend the whole night praying. They do not eat or sleep all night—only pray that God will help them in their new duties.

When dawn breaks, they bath and dress in long white robes. This shows that they promise to be pure and faithful.

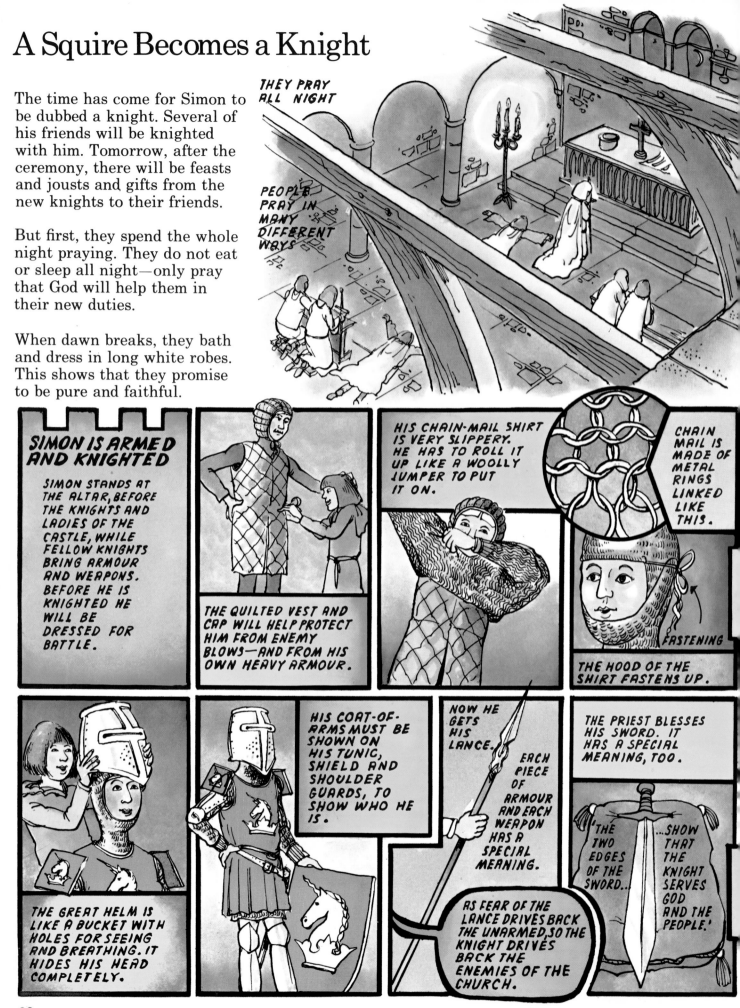

THEY PRAY ALL NIGHT

PEOPLE PRAY IN MANY DIFFERENT WAYS

SIMON IS ARMED AND KNIGHTED

SIMON STANDS AT THE ALTAR, BEFORE THE KNIGHTS AND LADIES OF THE CASTLE, WHILE FELLOW KNIGHTS BRING ARMOUR AND WEAPONS. BEFORE HE IS KNIGHTED HE WILL BE DRESSED FOR BATTLE.

THE QUILTED VEST AND CAP WILL HELP PROTECT HIM FROM ENEMY BLOWS—AND FROM HIS OWN HEAVY ARMOUR.

HIS CHAIN-MAIL SHIRT IS VERY SLIPPERY. HE HAS TO ROLL IT UP LIKE A WOOLLY JUMPER TO PUT IT ON.

CHAIN MAIL IS MADE OF METAL RINGS LINKED LIKE THIS.

FASTENING

THE HOOD OF THE SHIRT FASTENS UP.

THE GREAT HELM IS LIKE A BUCKET WITH HOLES FOR SEEING AND BREATHING. IT HIDES HIS HEAD COMPLETELY.

HIS COAT-OF-ARMS MUST BE SHOWN ON HIS TUNIC, SHIELD AND SHOULDER GUARDS, TO SHOW WHO HE IS.

NOW HE GETS HIS LANCE.

EACH PIECE OF ARMOUR AND EACH WEAPON HAS A SPECIAL MEANING.

AS FEAR OF THE LANCE DRIVES BACK THE UNARMED, SO THE KNIGHT DRIVES BACK THE ENEMIES OF THE CHURCH.

THE PRIEST BLESSES HIS SWORD. IT HAS A SPECIAL MEANING, TOO.

"THE TWO EDGES OF THE SWORD... ...SHOW THAT THE KNIGHT SERVES GOD AND THE PEOPLE."

AT DAWN THEY BATH AND DRESS.

THE CHEST PROTECTOR IS A NEW KIND OF ARMOUR, MADE OF METAL PLATES.

SHINGUARDS LEGGINGS

THE LEGS OF A MOUNTED KNIGHT ARE AN EASY TARGET, SO HE WEARS METAL SHIN-GUARDS AS WELL AS MAIL LEGGINGS.

THE ARM GUARDS AND SHOULDER GUARDS ARE TO SHIELD HIM FROM SLASHING SIDE-BLOWS.

THE TUNIC IS TO KEEP HIS ARMOUR FROM RUSTING IN THE RAIN AND SUN.

NOW BARON GODFREY GIVES SIMON THE KISS OF PEACE. THEN HE STRIKES HIM WITH THE FLAT OF THE SWORD.

AWAKE FROM EVIL DREAMS AND KEEP WATCH, FAITHFUL IN CHRIST AND PRAISEWORTHY IN FAME.

SIMON HAS BEEN DUBBED A KNIGHT.

NOW SIMON GETS HIS SPURS. HOLDING HIS SWORD, HE THINKS OF THE SWORDS OF THE GREAT HEROES — JOYEAUX, THE SWORD OF CHARLEMAGNE — EXCALIBUR, THE SWORD OF ARTHUR.

IT IS SIMON HIMSELF WHO KNIGHTS HIS GREAT FRIEND GERALD. THIS IS ONE OF HIS PRIVILEGES, NOW HE IS A KNIGHT.

AND NOW... ON TO THE FEASTS AND THE JOUSTING!

At the Scene of a Joust

Baron Godfrey has arranged a tournament to celebrate Simon's knighthood. The sun blazes on the lists—the fenced-off place where the knights will joust. Trumpets blare, to announce the arrival of the strange Black Knight. Simon has challenged him.

Today, for the first time, Simon has the chance to prove his skill in the joust—like his father and uncles, and like Roland and Richard Lion Heart in the minstrels' stories.

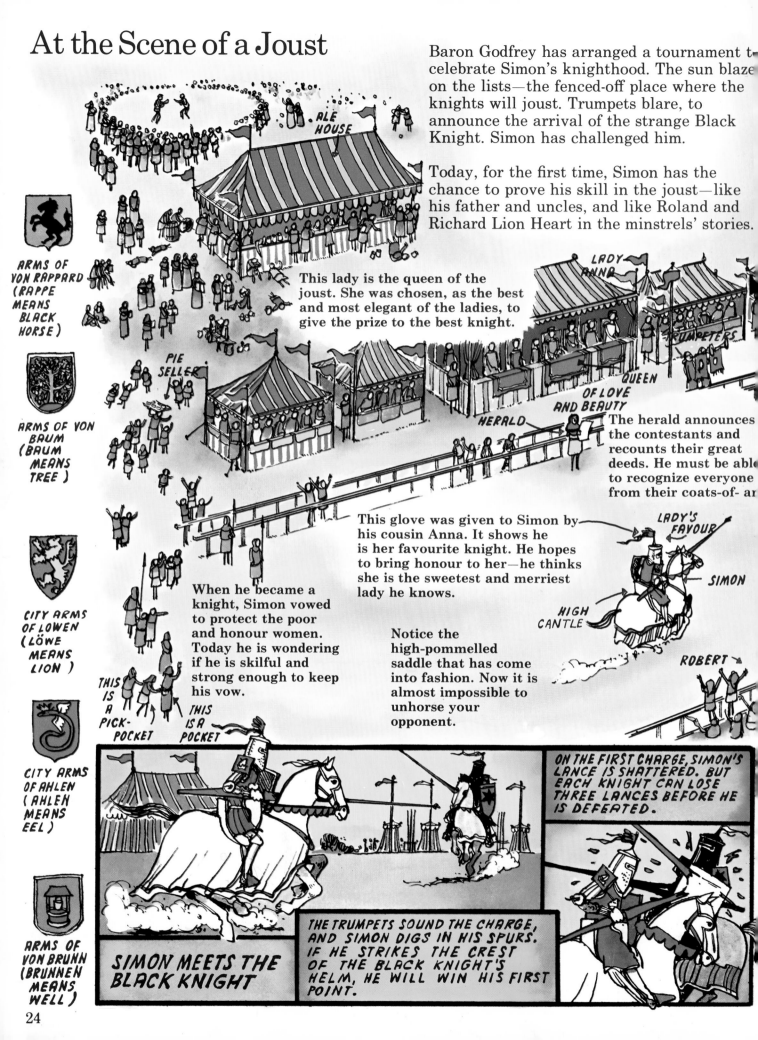

ALE HOUSE

ARMS OF VON RAPPARD (RAPPE MEANS BLACK HORSE)

ARMS OF VON BAUM (BAUM MEANS TREE)

CITY ARMS OF LOWEN (LÖWE MEANS LION)

CITY ARMS OF AHLEN (AHLEN MEANS EEL)

ARMS OF VON BRUNN (BRUNNEN MEANS WELL)

PIE SELLER

LADY ANNA

TRUMPETERS

QUEEN OF LOVE AND BEAUTY

HERALD

This lady is the queen of the joust. She was chosen, as the best and most elegant of the ladies, to give the prize to the best knight.

The herald announces the contestants and recounts their great deeds. He must be able to recognize everyone from their coats-of-arms

This glove was given to Simon by his cousin Anna. It shows he is her favourite knight. He hopes to bring honour to her—he thinks she is the sweetest and merriest lady he knows.

LADY'S FAVOUR

SIMON

HIGH CANTLE

ROBERT

When he became a knight, Simon vowed to protect the poor and honour women. Today he is wondering if he is skilful and strong enough to keep his vow.

Notice the high-pommelled saddle that has come into fashion. Now it is almost impossible to unhorse your opponent.

THIS IS A PICK-POCKET

THIS IS A POCKET

SIMON MEETS THE BLACK KNIGHT

THE TRUMPETS SOUND THE CHARGE, AND SIMON DIGS IN HIS SPURS. IF HE STRIKES THE CREST OF THE BLACK KNIGHT'S HELM, HE WILL WIN HIS FIRST POINT.

ON THE FIRST CHARGE, SIMON'S LANCE IS SHATTERED. BUT EACH KNIGHT CAN LOSE THREE LANCES BEFORE HE IS DEFEATED.

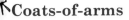

The field is crowded. People come from miles around—some to prove their skill, some to show their beauty, some just to enjoy the sports and feasts in the nearby fairground.

Simon's cousin Robert is at his side. He will arm Simon, rub down his horse, and come to his aid if he is injured—just as Simon did, when he was a young squire. Below you can see what happens when Simon meets his foe.

The ladies and nobles watch the jousts from splendid tents. They like jousts much more than tourneys which are muddled and brutal. In a tourney, two armies charge each other. There is blood and dust and noise. Men may be wounded and even killed.

DYING KNIGHT

The Black Knight is a knight errant. Most of his father's lands went to his elder brother, so he seeks his fortune at jousts. If he wins he gets the horse and armour of his foe. If he takes a rich knight prisoner he may get ransom money.

The young squires wait and watch, to see if they are needed. If a knight falls, only his own squire may help him.

SQUIRES

This knight was defeated in this morning's joust. He has lost his horse and armour, and he has spent his last penny to pay his faithful squire. Now he has nothing.

WOUNDED KNIGHT

DEFEATED KNIGHT

Coats-of-arms

An armoured knight has to wear a special sign on his shield and armour to show who he is. This is called a 'coat-of-arms'. At first these were simple. A knight picked almost any design he liked—perhaps a splendid beast or a picture that showed what his name meant. You can see some of them here.

Most people have only one name, like Simon, but they often have nicknames—like Simon from Strong Mountain ('Montfort' in French). Some coats-of-arms show these.

GRIFFIN WITH CROWN

SEA-HORSE

UNICORN

PEGASUS

ON THE LAST CHARGE, THE LANCES OF BOTH MEN ARE SMASHED. THEY DISMOUNT, TO CONTINUE THE DUEL WITH SWORDS.

AND THE BLACK KNIGHT IS DOWN. HE IS NOW AT SIMON'S MERCY. HE CAN BE STRIPPED OF HIS ARMOUR AND HELD PRISONER TILL RANSOMED.

BUT SIMON RELEASES HIM. HIS ONLY REQUEST IS TO EXCHANGE HORSES WITH HIS BRAVE FOE, AS A REMINDER OF THIS GREAT BATTLE.

Return From the Crusades

One day, a strange procession appears at the castle gates. Tanned, weary-looking men lead a ragged string of mules and donkeys, laden with baggage. Among the pack-animals is a creature none of the castle people have seen before. Everyone runs to look. Even the men look strange. There is something foreign about their clothes and saddlery.

It is hard at first for Lady Alice to recognize that one of these men is her brother Rudolf—back from his travels on crusade. He has been away for four years.

Below you can find out where the crusaders went and what they did.

What is a Crusade?

A crusade is a religious war. The most famous crusades, in the time of knights and castles, were wars in which Christian armies from Europe tried to conquer Jerusalem and the holy places where Jesus lived and died. Like all wars, of course, they really happened for more than one reason. They started in 1095.

For centuries, Christians had made pilgrimages to the Holy Land – the bit marked in red on this map.

650-950 PILGRIMS CAME FROM EUROPE

← EUROPE

MEDITERRANEAN SEA

JERUSALEM

THE PINK AND RED BITS BELONG TO THE ARABS

For a long time, the pilgrims were treated well by the Arabs who ruled the Holy Land. The Arabs had a different religion (they followed the teachings of the Prophet Mohammed), but they were very courteous people. They respected the beliefs of the Christians, and made them welcome.

However, in the 11th century, the Arabs were conquered by the Seldjuk Turks. Now the map looked like this. (Notice how the red of the Arab states has been eaten up by the yellow that marks the Turkish states.) →

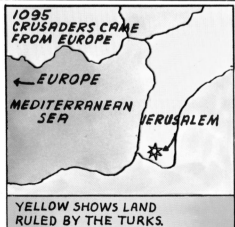

The Turks were also Moslems (followers of Mohammed), but they felt less sympathetic to the Christians. They made life hard for them, making them pay vast sums of money to see the holy city of Jerusalem.

Meanwhile, the people of Europe had really begun to want the goods that were brought from the Holy Land –particularly spices, which they used to preserve their food for the winter. So they were, for many reasons, very angry with the Turks.

When the head of the Christian church, Pope Urban II in Rome, demanded that they fight for Jerusalem, they were ready. This was the First Crusade.

The crusades continued for over two hundred years. Jerusalem was won by the Christians and then lost again. The map changed many times. In the end, Jerusalem stayed in the hands of the Moslems. But as you can see, the goods and stories brought back by the crusaders changed life for all Europe.

The Castle is Attacked

LORD JOHN HAS QUARRELLED WITH GODFREY. FOR DAYS THERE HAVE BEEN RUMOURS OF HIS BATTLE PREPARATIONS. NOW, IN THE DISTANCE, THE BANNERS OF JOHN'S APPROACHING ARMY ARE SEEN.

OLD AND CRIPPLED PEOPLE, WOMEN AND CHILDREN CROWD INTO THE WELL-STOCKED KEEP. LUCKILY, THERE IS EVEN A WELL IN THE BASEMENT.

ANNA HANGS BACK—SHE WISHES SHE COULD FIGHT. SHE THINKS OF THE WOMEN WHO BATTLED ALONGSIDE SIMON DE MONTFORT— AND THE LADY OF THE GOLDEN BANNER, WHO LED A GREAT ARMY ON CRUSADE...

ANNA

SHELTERS ARE BEING BUILT ON LOGS THRUST INTO SPECIAL HOLES IN THE WALLS. THIS WILL LET THE MEN-AT-ARMS POUR BOILING WATER AND DROP HUGE STONES ON ATTACKERS BELOW.

Siege Weapons

Often the most powerful weapons in a siege are food and water. If the besiegers are well-supplied and the castle is not, the besiegers can just sit back and wait. Sooner or later the defenders must starve or surrender. At other times the besiegers might give up—from bad food, illness, or boredom.

Both sides use other weapons to try to win more quickly— like the siege machines shown here. Most of these were used long ago by the Romans.

If the besiegers fill in the ditch round the castle, they can do lots of damage. For instance, they can roll a siege tower against the wall, raise its platform, and climb in.

SIEGE TOWER

Or they can tunnel under the wall and then burn the wooden props of the tunnel, so that the wall collapses.

IT IS NOON OF THE SECOND DAY. LORD JOHN'S MEN HAVE TUNNELLED UNDER THE CASTLE WALL. THE WALL CRUMBLES. THE DEFENDERS RETREAT.

IT IS NIGHT. UNKNOWN TO THE ENEMY, SIMON AND A GROUP OF KNIGHTS CREPT OUT OF A SECRET GATE (THE POSTERN GATE) AT THE BACK OF THE CASTLE. SILENTLY, THEY SET FIRE TO THE ENEMIES' SUPPLIES. THE ENEMY FLEES!

MANY HAVE DIED. EVEN BARON GODFREY HAS BEEN WOUNDED. BUT THE CASTLE IS SAVED.

...hey can batter down the wall ...ith heavy logs or special ...ttering rams.

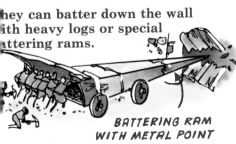

BATTERING RAM WITH METAL POINT

...hielded by mantlets, they can ...ring scaling ladders and try to ...limb the wall.

MANTLET

Most archers use cross-bows. A cross-bow takes a long time to load. You must use a winch—or two hands and a foot.

WINCH

STIRRUP

ARROW SLITS FOR CROSS-BOW

The English have learned to use long-bows. These can be shot much more quickly.

ARROW SLITS FOR LONG-BOW

Castle Map

This map shows where you can find some of the best-preserved examples of castles built about the time the events in this book take place.

FINLAND

NORWAY

SWEDEN

× Abo

Akershus ×

ESTONIA

× Visby

DENMARK

LATVIA

× Hammershus

LITHUANIA

Drum ×

× Marienburg

BELARUS

× Craigmillar

POLAND

Alnwick ×

Carrickfergus ×

IRELAND

BRITAIN

Trim ×

Conisbrough ×

GERMANY

CZECH
REPUBLIC

UKRAINE

Carlow ×

Caernarvon ×

× Castle Rising

Ferns ×

Harlech ×

× Muiden

Coburg ×

× Bezdéz

Leyden × HOLLAND

× Karlstejn

SLOVAKIA

× Chepstow

Château des Comtes ×

Tower of London ×

BELGIUM

Marksburg ×

× Eltz

× Ortenberg

Araberg ×

MOLDOVA

× Restormel

Arques ×

Falkenstein ×

AUSTRIA

× Viechtenstein

HUNGARY

Château Gaillard × × Gisors

LUXEMBOURG

La Roche Guyon ×

ROMANIA

× Etampes

× Pfeffengen

Angers ×

SWITZERLAND

× Kropfenstein

Langeais × × Loches

× Chillon

SLOVENIA

CROATIA

FRANCE

Trento ×

Fenis ×

Golubac ×

Sirmione × × Castelvecchio

BOSNIA-
HERZO-
GOVINA

YUGOSLAVIA

× Villandraut

Sarzanello ×

× Gradara

BULGARIA

Aigues Mortes ×

San Gimignano

MACEDONIA

Carcassonne ×

ITALY

× Burgos

CORSICA

Roumeli Hissar ×

× Castel Sant'Angelo

Castel del Monte ×

Anadoli Hissar ×

× Villalonso

× Avila

× Castel Nuovo

ALBANIA

× Amieira

SARDINIA

GREECE

PORTUGAL

SPAIN

× Bellver

× Lisbon

Monte Agudo ×

Palermo ×

Catania ×

SICILY

ALGERIA

TUNISIA

CRETE

MOROCCO

30

How Castles Grew

A castle is a fortress you can live in, protected from your enemies. The first kind of castle in Europe (before about 1000 AD) was a low tower, usually two stories high, with the living hall above the storerooms.

When people had to build quickly, as the Normans did after they conquered England, they sometimes built castles of wood. They often used a motte-and-bailey castle.

As you can see, the 'motte' is a mound. The 'bailey' is a fenced-off place that holds up invaders. Sometimes these were later replaced by stone castles.

TURKEY

SYRIA

⋇ Krak des Chevaliers

YPRUS

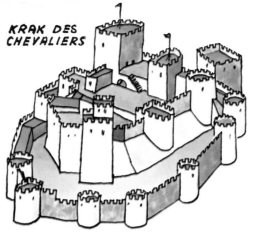
KRAK DES CHEVALIERS

The crusaders learned a lot about castle-building from the great castles they found on crusades, like the famous Krak des Chevaliers, in Syria.

CAERPHILLY

After this, many castles were built with several circles of walls (concentric castles) or other improvements, like towers along the walls (mural towers).

Castles grew a little differently in each place. For example, in mountainous parts of Italy, a castle might be just a tower built on a rocky peak.

COUCY

In France, many castles became luxurious homes for noblemen. Castles built by the Teutonic Knights of Germany had chapels within their walls.

And each castle, in each country, has its own special story.

Useful Dates

When you read history, it is useful to keep some dates in mind to help work out why certain happenings were important. These dates may help.

1 AD Birth of Jesus
AD (anno Domini) means 'Year of our Lord'. When our calendar was started, people thought Jesus was born in this year. At this time, the Romans ruled all round the Mediterranean Sea and in parts of Europe.

476 Fall of Rome
Warriors from the north had been fighting the Romans for centuries. At last they destroyed Rome.

732 Defeat of the Moslems by Charles Martel
The next conquering people round the Mediterranean were the Moslems. They conquered Portugal and Spain, but Charles Martel defeated them in France.

870 Danish Conquest Begins
Vikings from Denmark had been raiding Europe for years. Now they started colonies. Many of the ideas of knighthood were started by Europeans defending themselves against the Vikings.

1066 Norman Conquest
Vikings who had settled in Normandy (France) conquered Britain.

1095 First Crusade Begins
European Christians tried to conquer Jerusalem.

1150 First Paper Mill in Europe. Universities started (Paris and Salerno)
The crusaders brought back many inventions and ideas from the Moslems, who had big libraries, and universities where people exchanged knowledge.

1380 Bible Translated into English.
Until about this time, few ordinary people had a chance to read the Bible. When they did, many began to protest against the priests (argue that they were wrong). They became known as Protestants.

Going Further

Looking at Castles

At good bookshops you can buy maps of your area that show any nearby castles or castle remains. Try Ordnance Survey (1 to 50,000) or Bartholomews (1 to 100,000) maps.

To find the best castles, though, you need a guide book. *Historic Houses, Castles and Gardens Open to the Public,* published by Reed Information Services every year contains details of opening hours, prices and how to get there. Other general books include *The English Castle* published by Blandford Press and *Hudson's Historic House and Castle Directory.*

When you visit a castle, notice things like rivers and ditches and how the ground slopes, to work out where an enemy would attack. Sometimes you can only guess what the castle would have been like, long ago. Look for clues—like holes for beams in the walls.

Looking at Churches

Ask at libraries and tourist offices to find interesting old churches. On the arms of some very old choir stalls you can still see the scratch-marks where choir-boys once played games like draughts. Turn-up seats in choirs sometimes have very funny and interesting carvings underneath. Also, notice the dates carved in Roman numerals on the walls and grave-stones.

Books to Read

Look in the library for fact books, but try these books, too. The first three are paperbacks.
King Arthur and His Knights of the Round Table by Roger Lancelyn Green (Puffin)
The Adventures of Robin Hood by Roger Lancelyn Green (Puffin)
The Sword and the Stone by T. H. White (Armada Lion)
The Story of Mankind by Hendrik Van Loop (Harrap)

Consultants

Peter Vansittart is a novelist with a special interest in the 13th century. He is a former teacher and a distinguished writer on historical subjects.

Angela Littler has written and edited several best-selling children's information books.

Nicholas Hall specializes in medieval architecture, armour and weapons.

Gillian Evans is with the Medieval Centre at Reading University.

We would like to thank the Western Manuscript Department of the Bodleian Library at Oxford for permission to reproduce material from their collection on pages 4 and 5.

Index

abacus, 21
apprentices, 16, 19
Arabic numerals, 27
Arabs, 26–27
archers, archery, 6, 20
arches, 16–17
armour, 20–21, 22–23

banks, bankers, 18–19
barber, 18
barbican, 6
baths, 11, 23, 26
battering rams, 29
beds, bedrooms, 10
boars, 5, 6, 12, 15
bows and arrows, 20, 29
bread, 14, 15
bridges, 5
bucklers, 21

cathedrals, 2, 4, 16
cauldrons, 9, 14
chain mail, 22–23
children, 9, 10, 11, 13
Christianity, 26–27, and see
   Church, the; churches; friars;
   priests
Church, the, 2, 27
churches, 2, 16–17, 19, 32
coats-of-arms, 22, 24, 25
criminals, 8, 18, 19
cross-bows, 20, 29
crusades, 8, 18, 26–27
curfew, 18

dentists, 18
drawbridge, 6–7
dungeon, 8

education, 8, 19; of a knight, 20–21

falcons, 6, 12–13
farmers, farming, 2, 4
ferry, 5
fighting, 12, 20, 21; and see
   joust, jousting
fires, fireplaces, 8, 9, 18
food, 5, 8, 9, 12, 14–15, 20
forge, 7
friars, 2, 8

gardens, 9, 19
garderobe, 9
gatehouse, 6–7
gatekeeper, 18
glass, 8
goldsmith, 18
guilds, guildhall, 18

herbs, 9, 11, 14
heralds, 24
Holy Land, the, 26–27
hospital, 18
hunting, 5, 12–13, 20

Jerusalem, 26–27
joust, jousting, 21, 24–25

keep, the, 7, 8–9
keystone, 16–17
kitchen, the, 7, 8, 14
knights, 2, 4, 5, 8, 12, 20–23; at
   the joust, 24–25; education of,
   20–21; and knighting ceremony,
   22–23; knights errant, 25

ladies, 2, 8, 9; and clothes, 11; at
   the hunt, 12; at the joust, 24–25;
   laws and punishments, 2, 8,
   18, 19; long-bows, 29

market and market stalls, 18, 19
masons, 6, 16–17
meat, 8, 9, 14, 15
medicine, 9; and see surgeon, the
men-at-arms, 2, 5, 8, 10, 12
messengers, 5
minstrels, 2, 5, 15
money-lenders, 19
monks, 2, 11
mortar, 16, 17
mortar and pestle, 14
Moslems, 26–27
music, musicians, 2, 8, 12, 13, 15

numerals, 21, 27, 32
nuns, 2, 11

ovens, 7, 14

pages, 20
peasants, 2, 4, 5, 12, 19
pilgrims, 8, 19
pillory, the, 18
plays, 19
police, 8, 19
Pope, the, 2, 27
portcullis, 6, 7
priests, 2, 21

reading, 21
rivers, 5, 19
roads, 4, 5
Roman numerals, 21, 27, 32
Romans, the, 4, 5, 28, 31
rubbish, 18
rushes, 10

saddles, 24
salt, 8
sentries, 7
serfs, 2, 4

servants, 2, 8, 10, 11, 14
shields, 21, 22, 25
shops, shopping, 18–19
sieges, 6, 28–29
siege-weapons, 28–29
silk, 26
soap, 9, 11, 26
soldiers, 2, and see men-at-arms
spices, 8, 9, 14, 27
squires, 2, 15, 20–21; at the joust,
   25; knighting of, 22–23
stables, 6, 7
stewards, 2, 8, 18
sums, 21
surgeon, the, 18
swords, 21, 22, 23, 25

tapestries, 8
teachers, teaching, 8, 19, 21
thatchers, 6, 8
tournaments, 12, 24
tourneys, 25
town council, 19
towns, 16, 18–19
traders, 8, 15, 16
treadmill, 17
troubadours, 2, 8
Turks, 26–27

universities, 19
Urban II, Pope, 27

wages, 13
wars, 8, 12, 26
watchmen, 18
watermills, 4
weapons, 28–29, and see bows,
   lances, shields, swords
wolves, 5
writing, 21

The Time Traveller Book of PHARAOHS AND PYRAMIDS

Tony Allan
assisted by Vivienne Henry

Illustrated by Toni Goffe
Designed by John Jamieson

Contents

2   Going Back in Time
3   The People You Will Meet
4   A Trip to Ancient Egypt
6   Along the Nile
8   At Home with Nakht
10 Giving a Feast
12 Visit to a Temple
14 Going to School
16 A Trip to the Pyramids

18 Setting Sail for the Court
20 At the Pharaoh's Court
22 Battle!
24 A Warrior is Buried
26 The World of the Spirits
28 The Story of the Pharaohs
30 How We Know About
    Ancient Egypt
32 Index and Further Reading

Going Back in Time

There are plenty of ways of going back in time. You do it every time you go to a museum or a castle and try to imagine how people used to live many years ago. Or you can do it by looking at pictures and books. That is what this book is about.

It takes you on a trip back to the very beginning of history. The people of ancient Egypt were among the first to leave behind pictures and writings showing how they lived. It is by looking at them that we can know what ancient Egypt was like.

In this book you are going to make a journey back in time. It is as if you had been given a magic Time Helmet to take you to Egypt as it was over 3,400 years ago. On the next page are the people you will meet when you are wearing it.

The Time Travelling Helmet

This is the Magic Time Travelling Helmet. You can go back to any time you want, simply by setting the time and place controls. This time you are going to Egypt as it was in the year 1400 B.C.

This is Your Destination

Egypt is in the north-east corner of Africa, south of the Mediterranean Sea. You have to go back 33 centuries. Below are a few stop-off points to show you how things change when you jump back in time.

This is north-west Europe in 1940, before your parents were born. Things have not changed very much, but notice the aeroplane and the radio.

You have gone back another 40 years. Things are quite a bit different. There are oil-lamps, lots of decorations, and the women wear long clothes.

Now a big jump over 400 years. The only lighting is by candles, and all the heat comes from a big open fire. Most of the furniture is plain, and the window is made of tiny panes of glass.

This time you have moved in time and place, to Rome in 100 A.D. You have already gone back nearly 1900 years, but you still have almost as far to go again. Ancient Egypt is the next stop.

The People You Will Meet

The Egyptians all live within a few miles of the River Nile. It is warm and sunny most of the time, so they do not need to wear many clothes. Children hardly ever wear clothes at all.

The rich people have pleasant lives. They live on big estates, where servants and slaves do much of the work. But most of the people are poor peasants who must work hard to live.

Nakht is a wealthy landowner who lives in a big house a few miles up the Nile from the city of Memphis. He often has to go to the city, because, like his father before him, he is in charge of the lands of a temple there.

Tiy has been married to Nakht for twenty years. She is called Mistress of the House, and has to look after it and take care of the children. All the furniture and household goods belong to her.

The Pharaoh is the ruler of all Egypt. His subjects believe that he is a god in the body of a man, and think that he can do no wrong. He is so revered that people have to kneel down before they speak to him.

Mosi, their eldest son, is 16. His father wanted him to train as a scribe, but Mosi wants to be a soldier. Nakht has finally agreed to this, and has promised to introduce him to a general he knows.

Shery the eldest daughter, is a lively girl of 13. Because she is a girl, she does not go to school. But she is taught what she needs to know at home as well as singing and dancing.

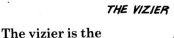

The vizier is the Pharaoh's chief helper. It is his job to see that the ruler's orders are carried out.

The youngest daughter is called Meu, which means 'kitten'. She is 8 years old. She has little to do but play in the garden all day.

Scribes earn their living by knowing how to read and write. Some work for the army, others in temples or on private estates. They organize the work other people do.

Hori, the youngest son, is 10. He is learning to be a scribe, and goes with his father to Memphis to attend the temple school. He expects to take over his father's job after Nakht has retired.

Ahmose, Nakht's nephew, is staying with his uncle's family. His own father has gone on a long trading voyage to Byblos, a port across the Mediterranean Sea in Lebanon.

Priests work in the temples, looking after the gods. They have to keep themselves pure and clean. They bathe four times a day, shave their bodies, and dress in the finest linen.

Most Egyptians are peasants. They have to work hard to grow enough food to live on, and have to pay taxes to the Pharaoh's officials. If they fail to pay, they are beaten. They normally have enough to eat, but when the harvest fails the Pharaoh sees that they are given grain from his Treasury.

Most of Nakht's servants are free to leave him if they want. But some are slaves. They are the children of foreigners captured in wars.

Soldiers lead hard, dangerous lives. But a few successful ones may become rich and famous generals.

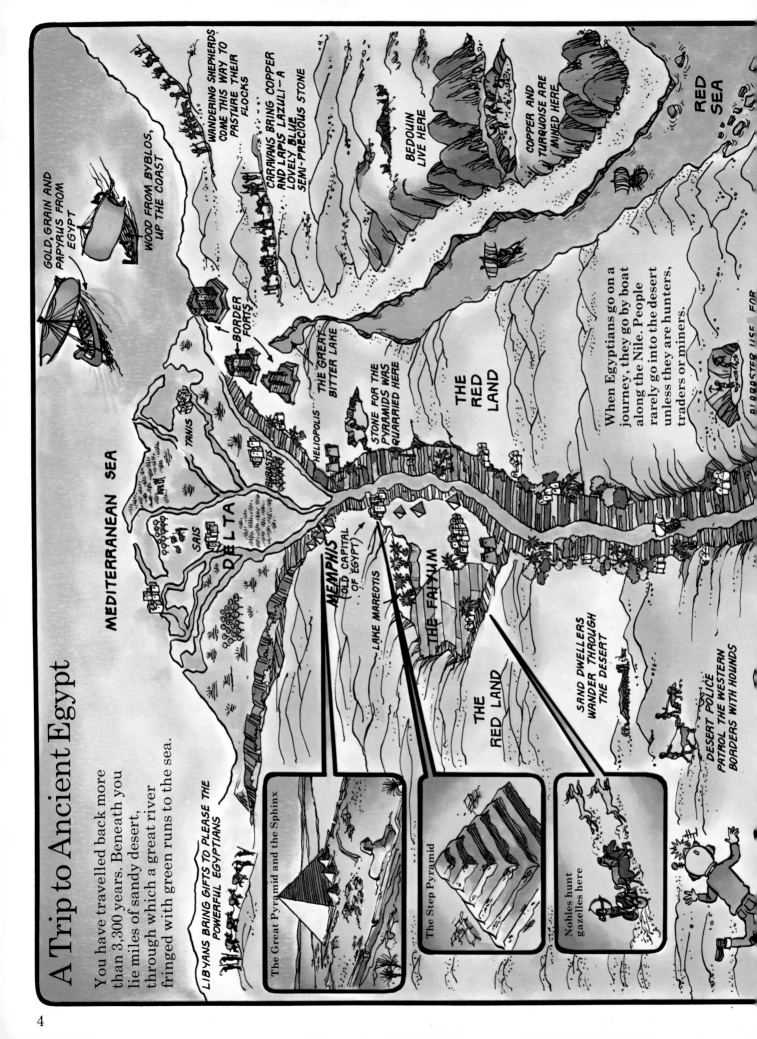

A Trip to Ancient Egypt

You have travelled back more than 3,300 years. Beneath you lie miles of sandy desert, through which a great river fringed with green runs to the sea.

LIBYANS BRING GIFTS TO PLEASE THE POWERFUL EGYPTIANS

GOLD, GRAIN AND PAPYRUS FROM EGYPT

WOOD FROM BYBLOS, UP THE COAST

WANDERING SHEPHERDS COME THIS WAY TO PASTURE THEIR FLOCKS

CARAVANS BRING COPPER AND LAPIS LAZULI – A LOVELY BLUE SEMI-PRECIOUS STONE

BEDOUIN LIVE HERE

COPPER AND TURQUOISE ARE MINED HERE

RED SEA

MEDITERRANEAN SEA

BORDER FORTS

THE GREAT BITTER LAKE

STONE FOR THE PYRAMIDS WAS QUARRIED HERE

HELIOPOLIS

TANIS

BUBASTIS

SAIS

DELTA

THE RED LAND

When Egyptians go on a journey, they go by boat along the Nile. People rarely go into the desert unless they are hunters, traders or miners.

MEMPHIS (OLD CAPITAL OF EGYPT)

LAKE MAREOTIS

THE FAIYUM

THE RED LAND

SAND DWELLERS WANDER THROUGH THE DESERT

DESERT POLICE PATROL THE WESTERN BORDERS WITH HOUNDS

The Great Pyramid and the Sphinx

The Step Pyramid

Nobles hunt gazelles here

4

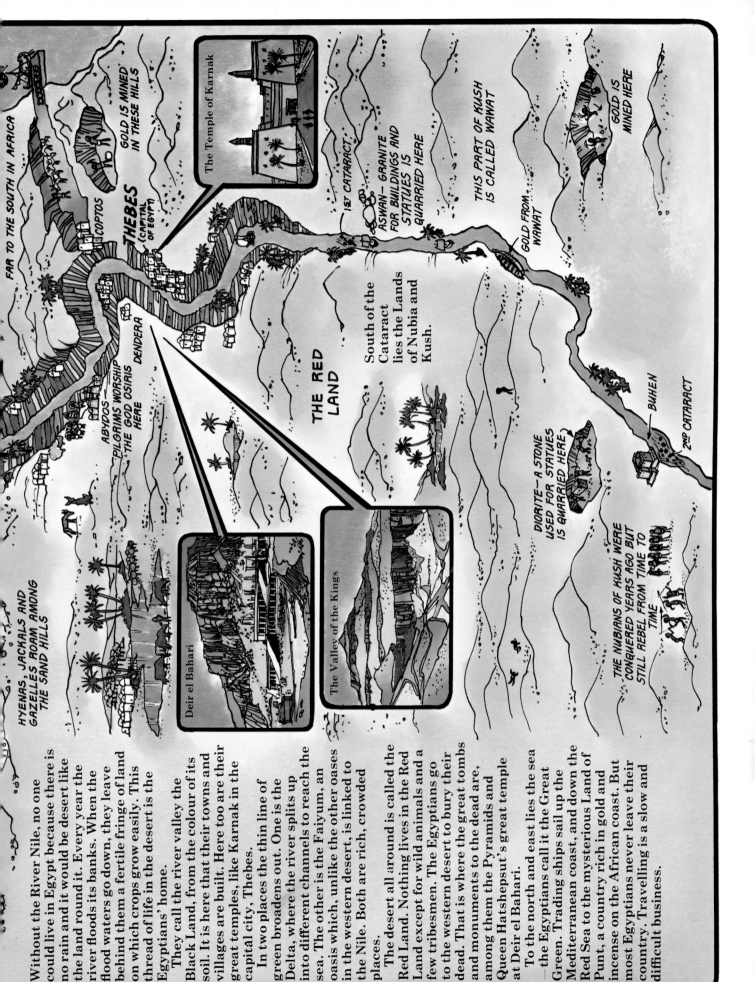

FAR TO THE SOUTH IN AFRICA

GOLD IS MINED IN THESE HILLS

COPTOS

THEBES (CAPITAL OF EGYPT)

The Temple of Karnak

1ST CATARACT

ASWAN—GRANITE FOR BUILDINGS AND STATUES IS QUARRIED HERE

THIS PART OF KUSH IS CALLED WAWAT

GOLD IS MINED HERE

GOLD FROM WAWAT

South of the Cataract lies the Lands of Nubia and Kush.

ABYDOS—PILGRIMS WORSHIP THE GOD OSIRIS HERE

DENDERA

THE RED LAND

BUHEN

2ND CATARACT

DIORITE—A STONE USED FOR STATUES IS QUARRIED HERE

THE NUBIANS OF KUSH WERE CONQUERED YEARS AGO BUT STILL REBEL FROM TIME TO TIME

Deir el Bahari

The Valley of the Kings

HYENAS, JACKALS AND GAZELLES ROAM AMONG THE SAND HILLS

Without the River Nile, no one could live in Egypt because there is no rain and it would be desert like the land round it. Every year the river floods its banks. When the flood waters go down, they leave behind them a fertile fringe of land on which crops grow easily. This thread of life in the desert is the Egyptians' home.

They call the river valley the Black Land, from the colour of its soil. It is here that their towns and villages are built. Here too are their great temples, like Karnak in the capital city, Thebes.

In two places the thin line of green broadens out. One is the Delta, where the river splits up into different channels to reach the sea. The other is the Faiyum, an oasis which, unlike the other oases in the western desert, is linked to the Nile. Both are rich, crowded places.

The desert all around is called the Red Land. Nothing lives in the Red Land except for wild animals and a few tribesmen. The Egyptians go to the western desert to bury their dead. That is where the great tombs and monuments to the dead are, among them the Pyramids and Queen Hatshepsut's great temple at Deir el Bahari.

To the north and east lies the sea — the Egyptians call it the Great Green. Trading ships sail up the Mediterranean coast, and down the Red Sea to the mysterious Land of Punt, a country rich in gold and incense on the African coast. But most Egyptians never leave their country. Travelling is a slow and difficult business.

Along the Nile

It is late in the year. The flooded waters of the Nile are going down. After three months with little to do, the peasant farmers are busy again, sowing seed for next year's harvest.

Another urgent job is to repair the canal banks. There is very little rain in Egypt, so water cannot be wasted. A system of catch-basins has been built, in which the flood overflow can be stored and used during the rest of the year to water the fields. It must not be allowed to drain away.

The river itself is busy with boat traffic. It is the land's main highway, and all heavy things, like statues and stone for building, are carried down it in sailing ships and barges.

People use it for private journeys too. The boat of Nakht, coming from Memphis, has just turned off the river. He is going home to the villa where he and his family live.

STATUE OF PTAH FOR A TEMPLE

FISHERMEN

Fishermen in boats made of papyrus reeds trawl the river for their dinner. There are many fish in the Nile. They make a tasty addition to a normal diet of bread and beer.

THE PHARAOH ROPE STRETCH REMEASURE FIELDS

NAKHT

WOODEN PICK

Canals are useful for travelling, and also because they carry water to fields far from the Nile. They must be kept in good repair.

Nakht is rich enough to have his own wooden boat. Wood is expensive in Egypt because not many trees grow there.

6

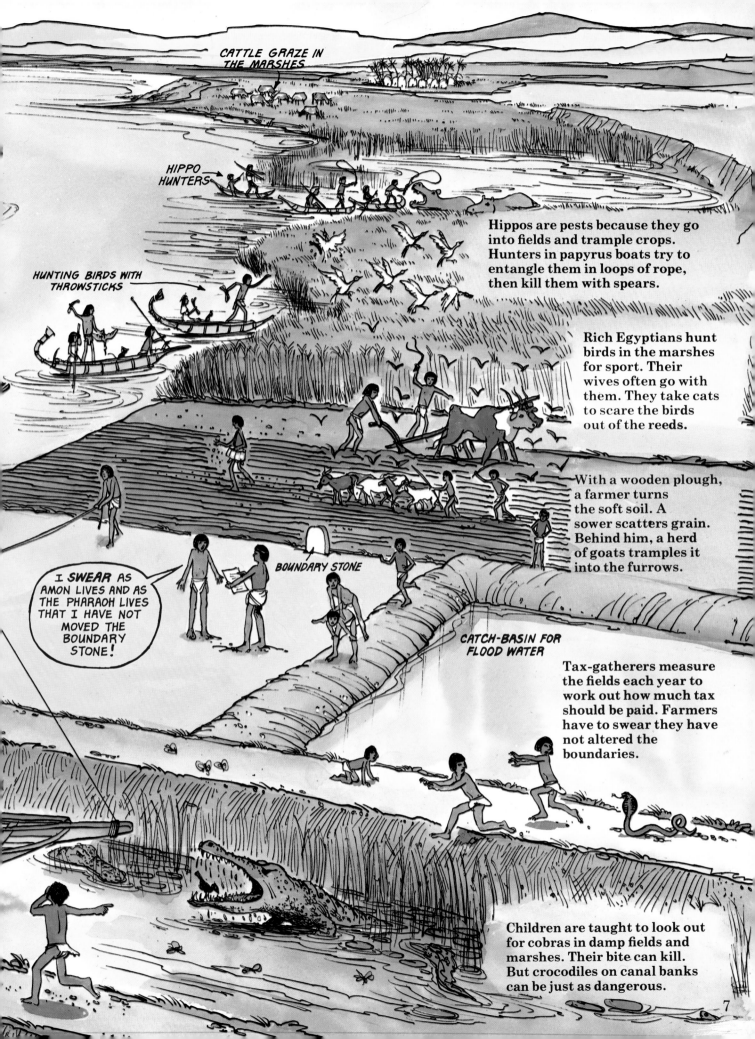

CATTLE GRAZE IN THE MARSHES

HIPPO HUNTERS →

HUNTING BIRDS WITH THROWSTICKS →

I SWEAR AS AMON LIVES AND AS THE PHARAOH LIVES THAT I HAVE NOT MOVED THE BOUNDARY STONE!

BOUNDARY STONE

CATCH-BASIN FOR FLOOD WATER

Hippos are pests because they go into fields and trample crops. Hunters in papyrus boats try to entangle them in loops of rope, then kill them with spears.

Rich Egyptians hunt birds in the marshes for sport. Their wives often go with them. They take cats to scare the birds out of the reeds.

With a wooden plough, a farmer turns the soft soil. A sower scatters grain. Behind him, a herd of goats tramples it into the furrows.

Tax-gatherers measure the fields each year to work out how much tax should be paid. Farmers have to swear they have not altered the boundaries.

Children are taught to look out for cobras in damp fields and marshes. Their bite can kill. But crocodiles on canal banks can be just as dangerous.

At Home with Nakht

Nakht has arrived home. He lives with his wife, Tiy, and their family on a large estate. He owns a house and garden, a stableyard, and outbuildings where the servants live and where food is cooked.

He also owns a lot of farming land nearby. Peasants look after this for him, and in return have to give him some of the food they grow. Nakht has a steward to help him look after the estate. His job is to see that the peasants give Nakht what is due to him.

Nakht's house is built of mud bricks, like all Egyptian homes. These are simply mud mixed with sand or straw, then left to dry rock-hard in the sun. The walls of the house are whitewashed. The floors are raised to make it hard for snakes to get in.

In the house, a ring of outer rooms surrounds a central hall. The hall's ceiling is raised, so high windows can let in light and air. It is cool and shady inside, but the family spend much of the day out of doors.

COLLECTING HONEY FROM BEEHIVES

The walled garden round Nakht's house is looked after and watered by his many gardeners and slaves.

NAKHT

TIY →

WORKMEN PICK FIGS WITH THE HELP OF PET BABOONS

Important guests are entertained in the pillared reception room.

STEWARD

SCRIBE

DUCKS' EGGS

Peasants from the estate bring cattle and geese to be counted by Nakht's steward. Those who bring fewer than they should are beaten.

8

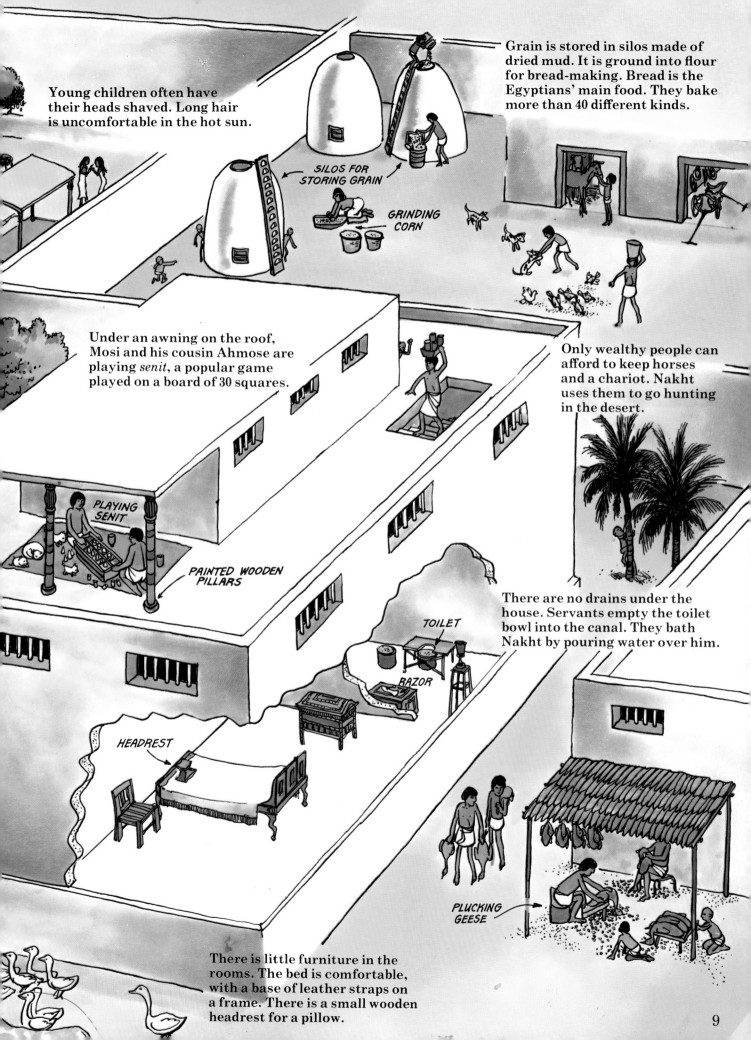

Young children often have their heads shaved. Long hair is uncomfortable in the hot sun.

Grain is stored in silos made of dried mud. It is ground into flour for bread-making. Bread is the Egyptians' main food. They bake more than 40 different kinds.

SILOS FOR STORING GRAIN

GRINDING CORN

Under an awning on the roof, Mosi and his cousin Ahmose are playing *senit*, a popular game played on a board of 30 squares.

Only wealthy people can afford to keep horses and a chariot. Nakht uses them to go hunting in the desert.

PLAYING SENIT

PAINTED WOODEN PILLARS

There are no drains under the house. Servants empty the toilet bowl into the canal. They bath Nakht by pouring water over him.

TOILET

RAZOR

HEADREST

There is little furniture in the rooms. The bed is comfortable, with a base of leather straps on a frame. There is a small wooden headrest for a pillow.

PLUCKING GEESE

9

Giving a Feast

Nakht has decided to give a feast to celebrate his return home. The Egyptians love parties, and never need much of an excuse to have one.

The guests are gathered in the central hall of Nakht's villa. Married couples sit together, but the unmarried are separated —boys and girls sit apart.

Singers and dancers entertain the guests, and servants bring round food. A lot of wine is drunk. Some guests drink so much that they have to be helped home.

All the guests wear perfume cones on their heads. These melt as the party wears on, drenching their wearers in sweet-smelling oils.

Servants pass to and fro among the guests, offering food and pouring wine. They give them flower garlands to wear round their necks and lotus blossoms to hold or wear in their hair. After the meal they will bring bowls of water for the guests to wash their hands in, because they eat the food with their fingers.

PET GOOSE

Preparing food

All the food for the feast is made by Nakht's servants. They make bread by kneading and shaping the dough, then baking it in flat cakes over a fire.

Ducks and geese are both favourite meat courses. The birds are roasted whole over an open fire. The cook fans the flames to keep it burning.

FIGS BREAD

HONEYCOMB

Plenty of fruit and vegetables are grown on the estate. Figs, dates and grapes are the favourites. Honey is used to sweeten drinks and food.

10

Shery gets ready for the feast

Before a mirror of bronze, Shery rims her eyes with a black powder called kohl.

She pounds red ochre into a powder to rub on her cheeks and palms.

Her servant hands her a wig. On top she puts a cone of perfume.

A blind harper waits to play when the dancing girls finish. His song is one of the oldest in Egypt. Make the most of time, he sings, for life is only a dream and all must die.

BLIND HARPER

WINE JAR

LOTUS BLOSSOM

PET MONKEY

Making wine

1

Most Egyptians usually drink beer, but rich people are also fond of wine. Most landowners have grapevines growing on trellises on their estates.

2

The grapes picked from the vines are taken to the press. While some workers trample them underfoot, others collect the juice that gushes out.

3

The grape juice is poured into pottery jars to ferment into wine. These are sealed with leaves and a cap of mud that bakes hard in the sun.

11

Visit to a Temple

The temple in which Nakht works is like a small city. It has its own workshops, school, library, granaries and storerooms. Outside its walls, which are built of stone, it owns many acres of farming land. Many people work for it, and depend on the food in its granaries and storerooms for their living.

The most important part of the temple is a small, dark room that only priests enter. It is the sanctuary where the god lives—for the Egyptians believe their temples are the homes of gods.

Ordinary people are not allowed to disturb the god. But they can go to the temple forecourt to make offerings to him. Or else they may go to the temple to work—like Hori. He has come to learn to read and write at the school.

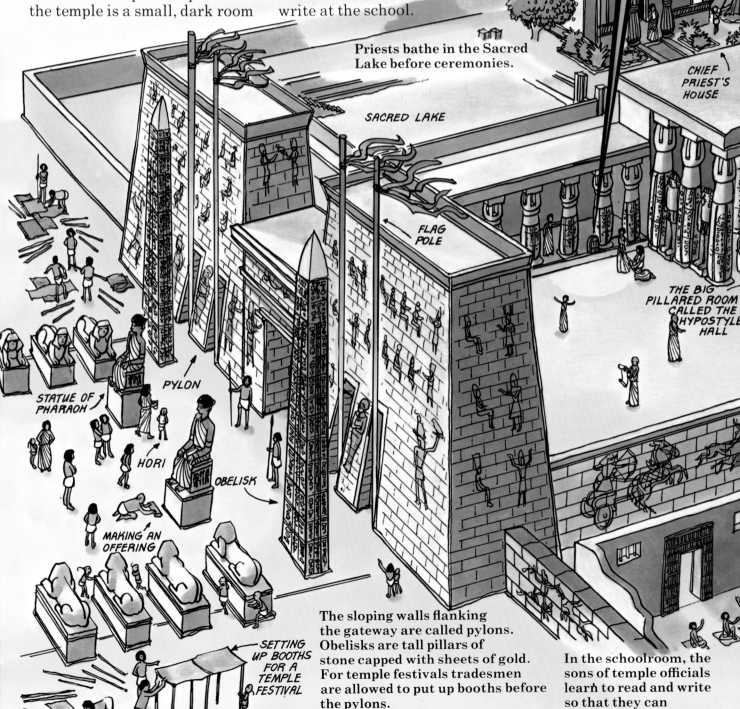

THIS IS A VOTIVE TABLET. PEOPLE BUY THEM TO OFFER TO THE GODS. THEY HAVE EARS TO HEAR THEIR PRAYERS.

Priests bathe in the Sacred Lake before ceremonies.

SACRED LAKE

CHIEF PRIEST'S HOUSE

FLAG POLE

THE BIG PILLARED ROOM CALLED THE HYPOSTYLE HALL

STATUE OF PHARAOH

PYLON

HORI

OBELISK

MAKING AN OFFERING

SETTING UP BOOTHS FOR A TEMPLE FESTIVAL

The sloping walls flanking the gateway are called pylons. Obelisks are tall pillars of stone capped with sheets of gold. For temple festivals tradesmen are allowed to put up booths before the pylons.

In the schoolroom, the sons of temple officials learn to read and write so that they can become scribes.

12

The Gods of Egypt

The Egyptians believe in many different gods. Once every city had a god of its own. Now there are some great gods, like Amon, whom all Egyptians worship. But people still feel loyal to the god who lives in the temple in their home town.

Here are three gods who are known in all the land.

AMON

Amon of Thebes is worshipped throughout the land as King of the Gods.

PTAH

Ptah, the god of Memphis, is the patron god of craftsmen.

BES

Bes, a comic dwarf god, brings good luck and happiness in the home.

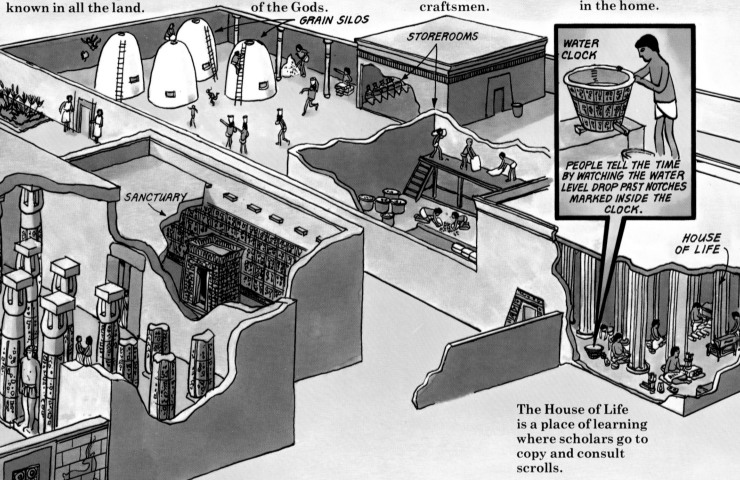

GRAIN SILOS

STOREROOMS

SANCTUARY

WATER CLOCK

PEOPLE TELL THE TIME BY WATCHING THE WATER LEVEL DROP PAST NOTCHES MARKED INSIDE THE CLOCK.

HOUSE OF LIFE

The House of Life is a place of learning where scholars go to copy and consult scrolls.

SCHOOL

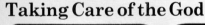

WOMEN MUSICIANS PRACTISING FOR THE FESTIVAL

Taking Care of the God

1

The main temple ceremony is that of looking after the god. Each morning a priest, newly shaved and washed, enters the sanctuary.

2

He takes the statue of the god out of its shrine. He sprinkles water on it, changes its clothing, and offers it food and drink.

3

He puts it back in the shrine and leaves the doors open until evening. He goes out of the sanctuary, wiping away his footprints.

13

Going to School

Most Egyptian children never go to school. As soon as they are old enough to work, the boys go to work with their fathers. The girls learn how to run a home.

Hori goes to school because he is going to be a scribe, like his father. Scribes are proud of being able to read and write, and they make sure that their sons can carry on the tradition.

Hori does not find school much fun. There are no sports or games. He spends his days doing copies and dictations, and chanting texts aloud. He also learns to do sums. His teacher is strict. Egyptian schoolmasters have a saying that a boy's ears are on his bottom—he listens when he is beaten.

To cheer Hori up, his father tells him that his knowledge will make him rich and successful. The texts he studies will teach him the wisdom of the past, so he will become a good man. When he has learned to write, he can study foreign languages, history, geography and religion.

Using reeds like paint brushes to sketch writing symbols, Hori and a schoolfriend take down a dictation. Papyrus is expensive, so beginners use bits of stone or broken pottery called ostraca to write on.

CANE

WATER JUG

INKSTAND

REED BRUSH

OSTRACA

RAG FOR RUBBING OUT MISTAKES

PAPYRUS SCROLLS

1 Making Papyrus

The Egyptians make many things from papyrus reeds, including rope, sandals, baskets and boats. They also use papyrus to make paper. The tall reeds grow in marshy ground. Workmen cut them down and carry them away in bundles.

In the workshop the long reeds are chopped into short lengths (a). The green outer skin is peeled away (b). A workman then cuts the white pith inside lengthways (c) into wafer-thin slices, using a knife with a bronze blade.

POUNDING MALLET

CLOTH

POLISHING STONE

Two layers of pith are placed crossways on a pounding block. Th[e] workman puts a cloth over them, and beats them into sheets with a mallet. To make a smooth writing surface, the sheets are finally polished with a stone.

Egyptian Writing

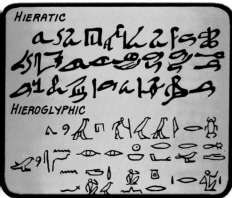

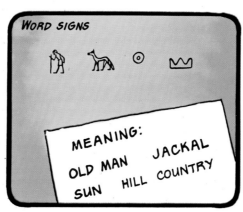
WORD SIGNS

MEANING:
OLD MAN   JACKAL
SUN   HILL   COUNTRY

SOUND SIGNS

HIEROGLYPHIC
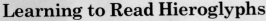

The Egyptians have two different kinds of writing—hieratic and hieroglyphic. Hieratic writing is a kind of shorthand, used for day-to-day business. Hieroglyphic writing, the older kind, is used for religious writings and for inscriptions on monuments. It is very difficult to learn.

As Hori will be a temple scribe, he has to learn hieroglyphic writing. Hieroglyphs are already about 2,000 years old. They were at first a picture language, in which there was a little drawing for each word. A small drawing of a boat meant 'boat'. It was quite easy to write simple messages.

As time passed, the writing became more complicated. Signs began to be used to stand for sounds, as the letters in our alphabet do. Words could be made up of several different signs. The picture above shows the main sound alphabet— but other signs are also used for groups of letters.

Learning to Read Hieroglyphs

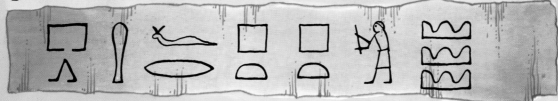

Hori spends a lot of time at school studying hieroglyphic inscriptions, to learn how to read the language. This one, like almost all of them, is a

mixture of sound signs and word signs. The Egyptians have no written vowels, so many words look alike. To help tell them apart, they often write

the sound of a word, then put a special sign, called a determinative, after it to make its meaning clearer.

Here is what the signs mean.

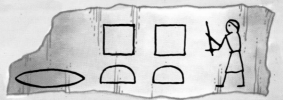
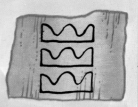

The word for 'house' sounds like the word for 'go forth', so the house symbol is used for both.

The walking legs show that here it means 'go forth'.

The club is a sound sign which means 'majesty'. The snake is the Egyptian letter 'f'. But it can also be used to mean 'his', as it does here.

The mouth symbol is the letter 'r' and, also, as here, the word for 'to'. The stool is the sound sign for 'p', the loaf of bread for 't'. Repeated, they spell the word for

'crush'. To make the meaning of the word clearer, a determinative sign for 'force'—a man striking with a stick—is tacked on at the end.

As Egypt is flat, the sign for 'hill' also means 'foreign land'. Here it is plural. The whole sentence reads: "Goes forth His Majesty to crush foreign lands."

KEY

WORD SIGNS AND DETERMINATIVES

(WALKING LEGS) GO
(MAN WITH STICK) FORCE
(HILLS) FOREIGN LAND

SOUND SIGNS

(HOUSE) STANDS FOR 'PR'
(CLUB) STANDS FOR 'HM'
(HORNED VIPER) STANDS FOR 'F'
(MOUTH) STANDS FOR 'R'
(STOOL) STANDS FOR 'P'
(LOAF OF BREAD) STANDS FOR 'T'

A Trip to the Pyramids

The pyramids were built more than a thousand years before Nakht was born. They are old and timeworn. Many of their outer stones have been stolen.

Yet they are still marvels. Most wonderful of all is the Great Pyramid of King Cheops, which stands on the edge of the desert across the Nile from Nakht's home.

During the flood season the waters of the Nile rise close to the Pyramid. Sight-seers like Nakht and his children can sail almost up to it, to pay their respects to the dead pharaoh and to visit the buildings.

1,200 Years Before—Building the Pyramids

One way of cutting blocks of stone for a pyramid was to cut notches in solid rock and then to hammer in wooden wedges. When water was poured on them they swelled, splitting off the blocks cleanly.

Most of the blocks for the Great Pyramid, weighing over two tons each, were quarried in the desert nearby. The white facing stones were carried on boats from the east bank across the Nile.

The ground where the pyramid was to be built had to be cleared of sand and stone. Workmen using ropes and sighting sticks dug channels which were filled with water to make sure the site was level.

The most difficult job of all was to raise the heavy stones into place. Most people think they were pulled up a huge earth ramp that was raised each time a new layer of stones was added.

When the pyramid was finished, the ramp was taken away. As the ramp went down layer by layer, workmen put white limestone facing stones on the jagged sides of the pyramid, to give them a smooth surface.

After many years' work, the pyramid was ready. When the Pharaoh died, his coffin was dragged up to the burial chamber inside it. Then the way into the pyramid was blocked and hidden.

Inside the Pyramid

The Great Pyramid is the biggest stone building ever built. It is made of more than two million huge blocks of cut stone. King Cheops had it built while he was still alive to keep his body safe after death. He stocked the burial chamber with treasures to use in the after-life—jewels and furniture, hunting equipment and food.

But despite his efforts, thieves have found their way in. There is nothing left inside the pyramid but the stone coffin in which he was buried.

SMALL PYRAMIDS FOR THE PHARAOH'S CHIEF QUEENS WERE BUILT BESIDE THE TOMB

A causeway links the mortuary temple to a second temple nearer the Nile. When the river is in flood, people can sail up to the lower temple. The dead pharaoh's body was carried to it by boat.

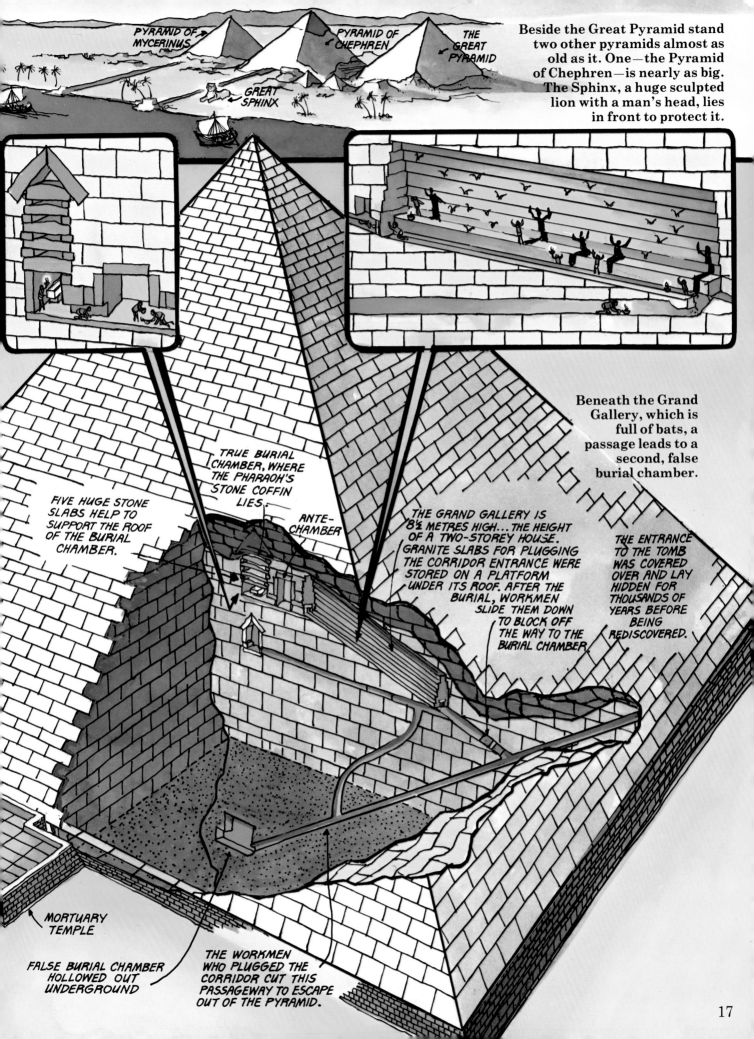

PYRAMID OF MYCERINUS

PYRAMID OF CHEPHREN

THE GREAT PYRAMID

GREAT SPHINX

Beside the Great Pyramid stand two other pyramids almost as old as it. One—the Pyramid of Chephren—is nearly as big. The Sphinx, a huge sculpted lion with a man's head, lies in front to protect it.

Beneath the Grand Gallery, which is full of bats, a passage leads to a second, false burial chamber.

FIVE HUGE STONE SLABS HELP TO SUPPORT THE ROOF OF THE BURIAL CHAMBER.

TRUE BURIAL CHAMBER, WHERE THE PHARAOH'S STONE COFFIN LIES.

ANTE-CHAMBER

THE GRAND GALLERY IS 8½ METRES HIGH... THE HEIGHT OF A TWO-STOREY HOUSE. GRANITE SLABS FOR PLUGGING THE CORRIDOR ENTRANCE WERE STORED ON A PLATFORM UNDER ITS ROOF. AFTER THE BURIAL, WORKMEN SLIDE THEM DOWN TO BLOCK OFF THE WAY TO THE BURIAL CHAMBER.

THE ENTRANCE TO THE TOMB WAS COVERED OVER AND LAY HIDDEN FOR THOUSANDS OF YEARS BEFORE BEING REDISCOVERED.

MORTUARY TEMPLE

FALSE BURIAL CHAMBER HOLLOWED OUT UNDERGROUND

THE WORKMEN WHO PLUGGED THE CORRIDOR CUT THIS PASSAGEWAY TO ESCAPE OUT OF THE PYRAMID.

17

Setting Sail for the Court

Mosi is going to Thebes. His father Nakht has had to go to the capital on business at the Pharaoh's court. He has asked his son to join him there.

Mosi is leaving from a small trading post on the Nile. The boat he is to sail in is returning to Thebes after unloading a precious cargo of goods from the Land of Punt.

The Pharaoh has sent this as a gift for a temple nearby.

The village is busy. Sailors are unloading the ship, while scribes weigh and note down its cargo. In the marketplace above the harbour, stall-keepers are doing good business. A group of wandering bedouin tribesmen have come in from the desert where they live to trade.

VENTS TO CA... BREEZES

LEATHER WORKERS

MOSI

BARBER

SCALES

BEDOUIN

Because it is warm out of doors, people work and shop in the open air. There is no money, so shopping is done by barter. To decide what costly goods are worth,

sellers work out their value in terms of fixed weight of gold, silver or copper called a *deben*. The buyer must offer something worth as many *deben* in exchange.

The bedouins' donkeys are laden with dyed woollen cloths to exchan... for food. The men have beards, and unlike the Egyptians they wear brightly-coloured clothes.

18

The cargo from Punt includes gold, elephant tusks (which will be turned into ivory ornaments), baboons, and incense trees for the priests to plant.

Egypt imports a lot of wood, because few big trees grow by the Nile. Most of it comes from Byblos, on the Mediterranean Sea's eastern coast.

TIMBER FROM BYBLOS

ELEPHANT TUSKS

SCRIBE

MIXING CLAY

BEDROLL

POTTERS AT WORK

KILN FOR BAKING POTS

Like the bricks of the houses, pots and jars are made from Nile mud. After an apprentice has trampled the mud into a paste, a skilled potter shapes it into vases that will be baked hard in the tall kilns.

Only wealthy people like Nakht have villas. Most people live in small, cramped houses with barely enough room for the family. In warm weather it is often more comfortable to sleep on the roof.

19

At the Court of the Pharaoh

Nakht has been ordered to attend a reception in the Pharaoh's palace in Thebes. Ambassadors from Syria are bringing tribute to the Pharaoh. Some of their gifts will go to Nakht's temple to honour the god Ptah.

Nakht is overcome with awe in the presence of the Pharaoh. Like all Egyptians, he worships his ruler. He believes he is the son of Amon. His word is law. It is an honour to be allowed to kiss the dust before his feet.

The young Pharaoh sits with his wife in the audience-hall. He behaves with the dignity expected of Egypt's ruler.

Yet secretly he is bored with the Syrians' flattery. He is more interested in Kush. He has heard rumours of a revolt, and is awaiting the arrival of his viceroy for the province. He knows that the news the viceroy brings could mean war.

The Syrians live in a mountainous land north-east of Egypt. They were conquered by the great Pharaoh Tuthmose III, and have been forced to send tribute to Egypt ever since.
Their envoys bring rich gifts, including a bear for the royal zoo. They also bring royal children to stay at court. Although the children will be treated well, they are hostages who will be killed if their parents rebel.

COPPER INGOT

A Day in the Life of the God-King

1 The Pharaoh's day begins early, because he has much to do. He is dressed by servants, and given the flail, the crook and the *nemes* head-dress—all symbols of royalty.

2 For Egypt to prosper, the Pharaoh must win the favour of his fellow gods. So he performs a ritual each morning in the temple, burning incense over an offering to Amon.

3 Much of the day is taken up with problems of government. Dispatches must be read and advisors consulted. The vizier helps to keep the Pharaoh informed.

20

The Crowns of Egypt

The Pharaoh wears different crowns for different occasions. This is the blue War Crown.

The White Crown is the crown of Upper Egypt. The Red Crown is the crown of the Delta region.

As ruler of all Egypt, the Pharaoh usually wears the Double Crown, which unites the Red and White.

The elaborate, top-heavy *hemhemet* Crown is worn only for temple ceremonies, if at all.

TRUMPETER ANNOUNCING VICEROY'S ARRIVAL

VICEROY OF KUSH

NUBIAN PRINCES

The Viceroy, whose official title is 'The King's Son of Kush', arrives with two loyal Nubian princes.

SCIMITAR

NAKHT

4 In the afternoon he goes to watch work on a temple he is building. The inside of the building is filled with rubble, over which the stone blocks can be hauled into place.

5 The Pharaoh enjoys going hunting, although this can be dangerous. The fiercest prey are lions. In ten years he has killed more than 100 of them.

6 Less tiring pleasures are waiting for him at home in the palace. Before going to bed, he plays a game of *senit*—a form of draughts—with his wife.

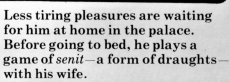

Battle!

The news from Kush is bad. Rebellious Nubian tribesmen in the far south have attacked a government outpost. The Pharaoh decides to send reinforcements to punish them.

An expedition is quickly organized. Most soldiers work in the fields in peacetime, so they have to be called up to fight. The crack soldiers are the charioteers, who have to provide their own chariots. But only a few will go to Kush. Carrying horses down the Nile on boats is difficult.

One of the soldiers called into service is Mosi. Although he is a new recruit, he has already been made a standard-bearer. He is eager for a chance to prove himself in battle.

1 The Pharaoh Calls the Men to Arms

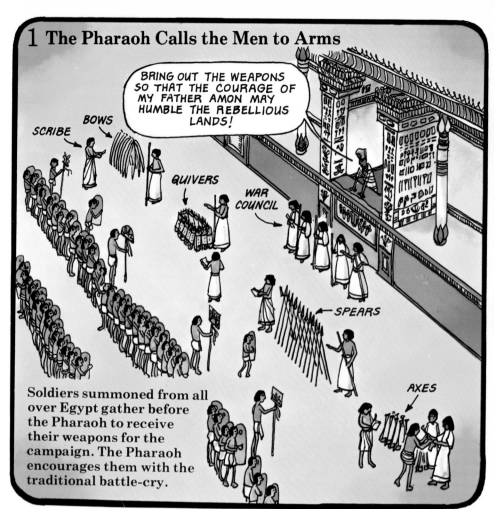

Soldiers summoned from all over Egypt gather before the Pharaoh to receive their weapons for the campaign. The Pharaoh encourages them with the traditional battle-cry.

2 The Expedition Camps by the Nile

The long journey down the Nile to the battlefield takes many days. Each night the army camps on the river bank. Generals have their own tents, with folding beds and stools, but the men have to sleep in the open.

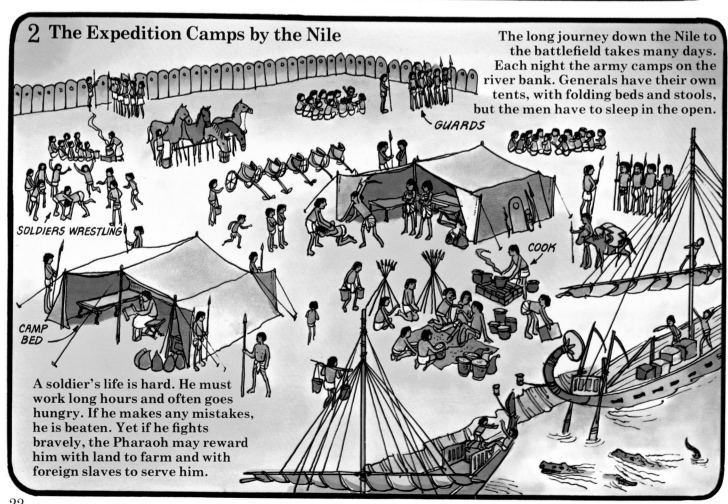

A soldier's life is hard. He must work long hours and often goes hungry. If he makes any mistakes, he is beaten. Yet if he fights bravely, the Pharaoh may reward him with land to farm and with foreign slaves to serve him.

3 Attack!

Archers begin the attack with a hail of arrows, then the foot-soldiers close in hand to hand. The Nubians, with their simple bows and clubs, are no match for the better-armed Egyptians. The fight is soon over. Then the chariots sweep by to chase the survivors from the field.

4 Spoils of Victory

Nubian captives are led away into slavery. Scribes count piles of hands cut from dead warriors—a grisly way of counting the enemy dead.

The Egyptian soldiers set fire to the Nubian encampment, and gather booty of food and animal skins.

A Warrior is Buried

The Egyptians won an easy victory in Kush, but some of their own soldiers were killed. One was a friend of Mosi's—a young Theban called Bata.

His grief-stricken parents have chosen to bring his mummified body back to Thebes for burial. They think he will be happier in the after-life if he is given a proper tomb.

The funeral procession makes its way to a tomb which his father had been preparing for himself. It is hollowed out of a cliff, west of the Nile.

Four priests—one of them wearing the mask of the jackal-headed god Anubis—perform the last rites over the mummy.

One priest 'opens' the mouth' of the mummy by touching its lips with a special tool. This is to give the dead man power to eat, speak and move in his next life.

MUMMY

WOMEN MOURNERS

FOOD FOR THE FUNERAL FEAST HELD AFTER THE BURIAL

CANOPIC CHEST

A big box called the canopic chest is put in the tomb with the mummy. Inside it are jars containing parts taken out of the dead man's body by the embalmers.

The women howl and throw dust over their heads. Some are relatives of the dead man, but others are professional mourners hired for the funeral. The men sit quietly and make little show of their sorrow.

24

1 Making a Mummy

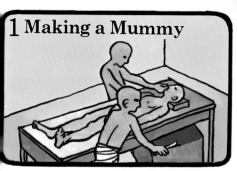

To keep the body in good condition for the after-life, embalmers have special ways of preserving it. They take the brains and some inner parts out of it. Then they clean it and fill it with sweet-smelling spices.

Next they cover the body with a white powder rather like salt called natron. Bags of natron are packed around the head. The body is left for many days, until all the moisture left in it has dried out.

The body is then washed and wrapped in linen bandages. It is coated with oils and resins and adorned with jewels and charms. A mask goes over the face. Finally it is wrapped again, ready for burial.

The bier is shaped like a boat in honour of the boat in which the sun god Ra travels across the sky every day. The dead man may meet Ra in the after-life.

Oxen drag the bier up the rocky paths on the Nile's west bank that lead to the Theban burial-ground.

BIER

FURNITURE FOR THE TOMB

The Egyptians believe that life after death is much like life before it. So they make sure tombs are stocked with furniture, food, and everything a man might need to enjoy his death in comfort.

25

The World of the Spirits

Every Egyptian hopes for a life after death in which he will work, eat and drink just as he did on earth. His tomb is his home for the after-life, so wealthy people like Bata's parents take great care preparing theirs. Dead people must eat, so piles of food are painted on most tomb walls. People believe that the painted food will, by magic, stop them from being hungry.

First the dead man must pass a terrible test. Nakht tells his children what will happen to Bata in the world of the spirits.

Whenever Egyptians go on a journey, they go by boat. They believe that the sun too must travel in a boat to make its daily journey across the sky. They believe that each night, after the sun has gone down over the western desert, the falcon-headed sun god Ra gets into another boat to sail over the world of the spirits.

Before he can live again, Bata must face a frightful ordeal. Like all dead people, he must go for trial before Osiris, the Lord of the Underworld. Only good people pass the trial; the rest are swallowed up for ever.

The Kingdom of Osiris lies in the west, where the sun sets. Bata will travel there by boat, just as his body went by boat across the Nile on its way to his tomb. The snake goddess Meresger will go with him to protect him from serpents in the other world.

The journey to the judgement hall, called the Hall of the Two Truths, is full of danger. Bata will have to pass through many gateways, each guarded by animal-headed gods armed with knives or with the feather that represents truth. To pass the gates he must recite the magic words written in his Book of the Dead.

Men fear death, yet every man can die knowing that he has a chance of a second life. When Bata died, his soul left his body in the shape of a bird. In daytime it can fly back to the land of the living to revisit the places Bata knew when he was alive.

A Plan of the Other World

Most wealthy Egyptians have books of magic called Books of the Dead placed in their tombs, to help them in the after-life. In them are drawings that show what people think the other world looks like. They are plans of the Fields of Yaru—the Egyptian heaven.

The plans show a peaceful land of fields and marshes watered by canals. Virtuous dead people live here among the gods of the spirit world. But they are also expected to work in the fields. This is less pleasant. To avoid having to do it, most rich Egyptians put small statues called *ushabtis* in their tombs. They believe that the *ushabtis* will do the hard work of farming the land for them.

3

In the Hall of the Two Truths, Bata must deny that he did any wrong in his life, before Osiris himself and 42 other judges. The

jackal-headed god Anubis will test his claim by balancing his heart on a scales against the feather of truth. A hideous beast

called the Devourer—part lion, part crocodile, part hippopotamus—waits to swallow him up if he has lied.

4

Ibis-headed Thoth, the scribe of the gods, will note down the result of the trials on his palette. If Bata lied, he would die for ever. But because he was

a good man, he will be taken by the falcon-headed god Horus to the throne of Osiris, to worship him. Then at last his new life in the Fields of Yaru will begin.

The Story of the Pharaohs

The story of the Pharaohs begins 5,000 years ago, in about 3,100 B.C. At that time a warrior king called Menes, from Upper Egypt, conquered the Delta lands of Lower Egypt. He built a new capital city at Memphis, and ruled over the two lands as the first of the Pharaohs.

It was at Saqqara, near Memphis, that the first of the great pyramids was built, 400 years after Menes's death, as a tomb for the Pharaoh Djoser. Before, Pharaohs had been buried in flat-topped brick tombs called mastabas. Djoser's tomb looked like six stone mastabas piled on top of each other. It is known as the Step Pyramid.

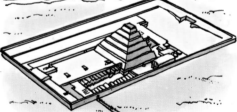

All the great pyramids were built in the next 400 years. The two built at Giza for Cheops and his successor, Chephren, were the biggest of all. They are still the most famous monuments of the Pharaohs, and they were built less than 500 years after Menes joined the two halves of Egypt into one land.

The age when the pyramids were built is known as the Old Kingdom. It was a time of peace and security. Egypt had no powerful foreign rivals to threaten her. The Pharaoh reigned supreme, and the country grew rich. The peasants farmed the land, the priests worshipped the gods. The rich nobles contented themselves with serving the Pharaoh, with looking after their estates and with hunting.

It was the nobles who finally brought the Old Kingdom to an end. They grew so powerful that they no longer respected the Pharaohs at all. The country was split in two and ruled by rival kings, one in the south and one in the north.

This time of troubles lasted for more than 150 years. It came to an end when a new family from Thebes managed to re-unite the land. Peace was restored, and the power of the nobles was checked. This new period of calm is called the Middle Kingdom.

The Middle Kingdom was the second great age of Egypt. It was a time of big engineering exploits, like the draining of the marshy Faiyum. Many of the finest hieroglyphic writings were composed then. Trading ships sailed the Red Sea and the Mediterranean. In the eastern Delta and in Nubia, chains of great fortresses were built to guard Egypt's borders and to protect her troops.

After two and a half centuries of peace, the country was again torn by civil war. The northern and southern halves split, and foreigners, invading from the east, conquered Lower Egypt. The Egyptians called them the Hyksos. They brought with them new weapons, including horses and chariots.

The Hyksos never conquered Thebes. After a century, the rulers of Upper Egypt managed to drive them out of the country by using their own weapons against them. Thebes became the capital of a re-united Egypt. The Theban Pharaohs won back the country's earlier frontiers. Inside Egypt order was restored.

During the first century of the New Kingdom, Egypt had something it had never had before: an effective woman ruler. Queens had reigned before, but only briefly and with little real power. Hatshepsut, however, as regent for her stepson Tuthmose III, took all the power of the Pharaoh for herself. She ruled the country well for 20 years, and built as a monument to herself one of the most wonderful buildings of all Egypt, the temple built into the cliff face at Deir el Bahari.

When Tuthmose III finally took power, the first thing he did was to try to wipe out the memory of the woman who had usurped his powers. He then set out to attack Egypt's enemies abroad. In 15 or more campaigns he built an empire that stretched from Syria to the Sudan. For the first time in her history, Egypt became a great warrior nation.

The empire he built lasted until the end of the long reign of his great-grandson, Amenophis III. It began to crumble under Amenophis's successor, who took the name Akhenaten. Akhenaten was the most revolutionary Pharaoh Egypt ever had. He moved the capital of the land from Thebes to a new city built in the desert, called Akhetaten. Above all, he tried to overthrow the old gods of Egypt, and to replace them with one god, Aten, the Sun's disk.

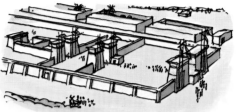

All his efforts were in vain. The religious revolution was stopped during the reign of the boy king Tutankhamen. Amon and all the other gods were worshipped again. Tutankhamen died at the age of 20, but other Pharaohs carried on the work. His successors did their best to wipe Akhenaten's name from people's memories.

In the interval since Amenophis III's reign, Egypt's enemies abroad had grown stronger. It took all the efforts of the last rulers of the New Kingdom to keep them in check. New powers challenged the Pharaoh's armies. They were the Hittites, from what is now Turkey, with whom Rameses II signed a treaty after a long war; and the Sea Peoples of the Mediterranean, defeated in a great naval battle by Rameses III, Egypt's last great warrior king.

After the death of Rameses III, Egypt's great days were over. The country grew gradually weaker as waves of invaders attacked it. The Nubians, subjects of the Egyptians for more than a thousand years, were the first to come. Then it was the turn of the Assyrians, who sacked Thebes in 661 B.C. From time to time strong rulers managed to halt the decay, but never for long. Egypt's next conquerors were the Persians. They were so hated that when Greece's Alexander the Great invaded Egypt to defeat them, he was welcomed as a hero.

After Alexander died, one of his generals, called Ptolemy, took power. He and his heirs ruled Egypt for the next 300 years. The last of the Ptolemys, and the last of the Pharaohs, was the famous Cleopatra. When she killed herself rather than submit to the Roman Octavian, the land became a province of the Roman Empire.

The way of life of ancient Egypt gradually disappeared. Even the great temples fell into decay. Yet its heritage did not die. It had given much to the world, from building and farming to writing and science. Other peoples were able to build on the foundations it left.

29

How We Know About Ancient Egypt

After Egypt became a part of the Roman Empire in 30 B.C., its old way of life came to an end. The people began to worship new gods, and the secrets of hieroglyphic writing were forgotten. Over the centuries, the old temples and palaces became ruins and were covered with sand and rubble.

In the 18th century, travellers from Europe began to take an interest in the past. They went to Egypt to explore the ruined buildings. People began to study hieroglyphics and learned once more how to read them.

Then archaeologists began to dig up the temples and tombs. They learned what Egyptian buildings used to look like, and found wall paintings, scrolls, and objects used in daily life.

People have used all these discoveries like pieces of a jigsaw puzzle, to build up a picture of how the ancient Egyptians lived. The picture is still not complete, but each new find that is made helps to fill the gaps in our knowledge.

This is what the temple of Abu Simbel looked like 150 years ago. The four great statues of Rameses II, for whom it was built, were half covered by earth and sand. Many other famous Egyptian monuments were completely hidden until archaeologists uncovered them.

The first explorers were only interested in spectacular finds, like this huge sculpture of Pharaoh Rameses II. It was dragged to the Nile, then taken to Europe. Early archaeologists did much damage to the buildings that they ransacked in search of treasure. Some even broke open sealed tombs with battering-rams.

How the Hieroglyphic Code was Cracked

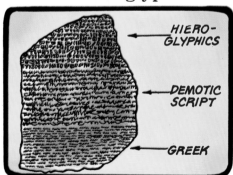

The vital clue to the meaning of the lost language was a stone dug up near Rosetta, in the Delta, in 1799. A message was written on it in Greek and in two kinds of Egyptian writing—including hieroglyphic.

A French scholar called Jean-François Champollion compared the hieroglyphs with the Greek text, which he understood. He worked for 14 years before he made out the meaning of a single word.

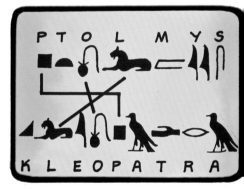

The first word he recognized was 'Ptolemy'—the name of the Greek Pharaohs. By comparing it with the spelling of 'Cleopatra' he worked out the symbols for the letters 'p', 'l' and 'o'.

Archaeological Triumph—Tutankhamen's Tomb

The finding of the tomb of the boy Pharaoh Tutankhamen, with most of its treasures inside, was the greatest archaeological discovery of all. It was also a triumph for a new kind of archaeology, very different from the slapdash methods of the early treasure-hunters.

It was found by a patient and determined Englishman called Howard Carter. From what he knew about royal tombs, he was sure that there must still be some undiscovered ones in the Valley of the Kings. With the help of money given by Lord Carnarvon, a wealthy nobleman, he began his search for them.

He worked for five years without finding anything Lord Carnarvon was ready to give up. Carter persuaded him to give the money for one last season's digging. This time, after only four days' work, Carter's men came across steps leading down into the ground.

It did not take very long to dig up the entry to the tomb. Three weeks after the first step was found, Carter made the first opening in the wall blocking up the burial rooms. Holding a candle through it, he peered into the darkness. "Can you see anything?" Lord Carnarvon asked. "Yes," he replied. "Wonderful things."

In fact there were more than 2,000 separate things in the tomb's four rooms, many of them made of gold, like the king's death mask.

On November 4, 1922, Carter first saw the entrance to Tutankhamen's tomb. His workmen uncovered a step while digging under some buried huts. Carter guessed at once that they had found what he had been looking for.

These were the first treasures that Carter saw when he opened the tomb. He later described seeing "strange animals, statues and gold—everywhere the glint of gold." In the centre was a gilded couch shaped like a cow.

This death mask of Tutankhamen was found on his body.

Index

Abu Simbel — 30
After-life — 25, 26–27
Archaeology — 30–31

Beds — 9
Bedouin — 4, 18
Boats — 6, 18–19, 26
Book of the Dead — 26–27
Building methods — 16, 21
Burial — 16, 24–25
Byblos — 3, 4, 19

Canals — 30
Canopic chests — 6
Carnarvon, Lord — 24
Carter, Howard — 31
Catch-basins — 31
Champollion, J.-F. — 6–7
Chariots — 9, 22–23, 28
Cities — 4–5
  Memphis — 4–5, 28
  Thebes — 4–5, 18, 20, 28–29
Cleopatra — 29–30
Crowns — 20–21

Dancers — 11, 24
Deir el Bahari — 5, 29

Faiyum — 4–5, 28
Farming — 7
Feasts — 10–11
Fields of Yaru — 27
Fishermen — 6
Food — 6, 9, 10

Games — 9, 21
Gods — 13, 26–27
Grain silos — 9, 13

Hittites — 29
Horses — 22, 28
House of Life — 13
Houses — 8, 19
Hunting — 9, 21
  birds — 7
  hippos — 7
  lions — 21
Hyksos — 28
Hypostyle hall — 12

Kush — 5, 20

Land of Punt — 5, 18–19

Make-up — 10–11
Mastabas — 28
Mourners — 24
Mud bricks — 8
Mummies — 25, 26

Nile — 4–5, 6–7, 18–19
Nubians — 5, 21, 23, 29

Obelisks — 12
Ostraca — 14

Papyrus — 14
Persians — 29
Pharaohs — 3, 18, 20–21, 22, 28–29
Potters — 19
Priests — 3, 12–13, 25
Ptolemy — 29, 30
Pylons — 12
Pyramids — 16–17, 28
  Great Pyramid — 4, 16–17, 28
  Pyramid of Chephren — 17, 28
  Step Pyramid — 4, 28

Rameses II — 29, 30
Romans — 29, 30
Rosetta Stone — 30

Sacred lakes — 12
Schools — 13, 14
Scribes — 3, 14, 19, 22
Sea Peoples — 29
Servants — 3, 8
Shopping — 18
Singers — 11
Slaves — 3, 22
Soldiers — 3, 22–23
Sphinx — 4, 17
Syria — 20

Temples — 12–13, 20
Toilets — 9
Tombs — 17, 24, 21, 31
Trade — 4–5, 18–19, 28
Tutankhamen — 29, 31

Ushabtis — 27

Valley of the Kings — 5, 31
Vizier — 3, 20
Votive tablets — 12

Warfare — 22–23
Water clocks — 13
Weapons — 22–23
Wine — 11
Wood — 6, 19
Writing — 14–15
  Demotic script — 30
  Hieratic script — 15
  Hieroglyphics — 15, 30

Further Reading

The Ancient Egyptians, Young Researcher Series (Heinemann Educational Books, 1992)

Pyramids, I Was There Series (Bodley Head, 1991)

Mummy, Eyewitness Guides Series (Dorling Kindersley, 1993)

Into The Mummy's Tomb (on Tutankhamen) Time Quest Series (Scholastic Children's Books, 1993)

Boy Pharaoh, Tutankhamen by Noel Streatfield (Michael Joseph)

Acknowledgements

This book was prepared in consultation with; W.V. Davies, Assistant Keeper of Egyptian Antiquities for the British Museum; and Dr Anne Millard, author of several books and articles on ancient Egypt, including *The Egyptians* (Macdonald), for children.

First published in 1977 by Usborne Publishing Ltd Usborne House 83-85 Saffron Hill London EC1N 8RT England

Copyright © 1993, 1990, 1977 Usborne Publishing Ltd.

Printed in Belgium UE

The Time Traveller Book of VIKING RAIDERS

Anne Civardi and James Graham-Campbell

Illustrated by Stephen Cartwright
Designed by John Jamieson

Consultant: Dr. D. M. Wilson
Director of the British Museum

Contents

2 Going Back in Time	18 Cousin Olaf Dies
3 The People You Will Meet	20 Björn Sails to Iceland
4 Earl Knut's Farm	22 Sven Goes Trading
6 Inside the Longhouse	24 Björn Settles in Iceland
8 Building a New Warship	26 A Meeting of the Thing
10 The Raiders Get Ready	27 A Winter Festival
12 Setting Off	28 The Vikings' World
14 Raiding a Monastery	30 The Story of the Vikings
16 A Big Feast	32 Index and Further Reading

Going Back in Time

This book is for everyone who would like to travel back in time. You have probably tried to imagine how people used to live many years ago. Now we have invented a Magic Time Travelling Helmet to help you.

By putting on the Magic Helmet and pressing all the right buttons, you can go back to any time you want. This time you are going back over 1,000 years to Norway—the home of the Viking Raiders.

On the next page are the people you will meet on your trip. They are not real people. But the things they do are things real people have done. Below you can see how to work the Magic Time Travelling Helmet.

Put on the Helmet

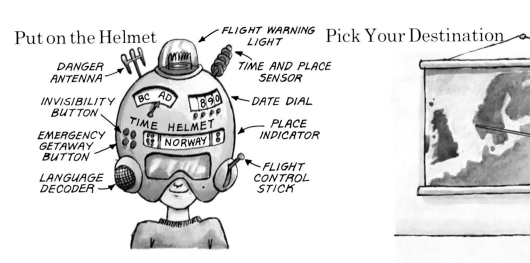

Pick Your Destination

Here is your Magic Helmet. You can see it has many useful gadgets to help you travel back in time.

With it, your journey to visit the Vikings, more than ten centuries ago, only takes a few seconds.

You are almost ready. Set the place dial to 'southern Norway' and the date dial to '890 A.D.'.

Below are a few stop-offs you might pass on the way to give you an idea of how things change.

Your first stop is in 1940, before your parents were born.

Things have not changed very much, but notice the aeroplane and old radio.

Now a jump of 40 years— things have changed a lot. There are gas lamps, no

electricity, a funny telephone and a lot of decorated furniture.

Back another 300 years— the room is lit by candles and heated by a log fire.

Notice the furniture and the small window with lots of tiny panes of glass.

Now we are at the time when people live in big, cold castles. There is no

chimney for the fire, nor glass for the windows. Next stop—Norway.

2

The People You Will Meet

It is a hard life for the people you will meet in Norway. The winters are long and cold and it is difficult to grow good food. Most of the men are fierce warriors. In the summer, they sail across the sea to raid and loot other countries.

EARL KNUT

SVEN

ROLLO THE BLACKSMITH

Earl Knut is the most important chieftain in this part of Norway. He owns a lot of land which he farms with the help of his eldest son, Eric, and many slaves. Knut is very rich—he often goes raiding in Britain and Ireland to steal treasure and capture slaves. Although he is a fierce man, he is kind to his wife and children.

Sven, the second son, is 21. He is wild and brave and enjoys going on raids with his father. One day he wants to be rich and famous too. He is also a trader and sells soapstone bowls, stolen treasure and slaves at the big trading towns down the coast.

Rollo, who is an old man now, comes from Rogaland in western Norway. He is the most important freeman on Earl Knut's farm. Rollo is a very skilled blacksmith and also makes fine jewellery. As well as weapons for the raiders, he makes farm tools, ship-building tools and pots and pans.

ASTRID

BJÖRN

LEIF

Astrid has been married to Knut for 24 years. When she was younger she went with him on his travels. Now, while he is away raiding, she stays at home and looks after the farm. Astrid is always busy spinning and weaving. She is a very good cook and brews strong beer.

Björn, the youngest son, is 19. His name means 'bear', but he is not really as strong and fierce as his brothers. Knut has given him a ship to take his family to settle in Iceland with some of their friends. Björn wants to find new land where he can have his own farm.

Leif is learning to be a blacksmith and helps Rollo in the smithy. He has a very bad temper which often gets him into trouble.

COUSIN OLAF

FREYDA

Freyda, the eldest daughter, is 16. Soon she will be married. Her mother is busy teaching her to cook, spin, weave and brew beer— all the things she needs to know to become a good wife. Freyda also helps to look after her two young sisters. There are no schools for them to go to—even their father cannot read or write.

Olaf, Earl Knut's first cousin, is also an important chieftain who owns a big farm and a longship for raiding. People call him Olaf Strongarm because he is famous for his great strength. When he was young, Olaf won many wrestling and weight-lifting competitions.

ERIC KNUTSSON

FREEMEN

SLAVES

Eric is 22 years old. Because he is the eldest son, he will take over his father's farm when he dies. Eric is called Knutsson, which means 'son of Knut'.

Many freemen work on Earl Knut's farm. They do not have their own land but the Earl has allowed them to build their own houses. In return, they help him to farm, build ships, smelt iron ore and carve soapstone.

Slaves do all the dirtiest and nastiest work on the farm. At the moment, Knut has twelve slaves. But when he next goes raiding he will probably capture more. His slaves are never allowed to carry any weapons

Earl Knut's Farm

You have jumped back in time to the year 890 A.D. With the help of the Magic Helmet, you have landed on Earl Knut's farm on the shores of southern Norway. The long, cold winter is over and everybody is busy working on the land. There is lots to be done now that the snow has melted.

The Earl lives here with his wife Astrid, their six children and all their grandchildren. Astrid's aunt and her family live with them too.

Knut has many slaves and freemen to help him grow food, and to look after his cows, sheep and horses. All the slaves live together in a small, stone hut close to the main house, called the longhouse. The freemen have come from their houses on the Earl's land. Some of their wives and children help Astrid with the housework and cooking in Knut's longhouse.

These men are breaking up soapstone, a kind of soft rock, to make into bowls, lamps and fishing weights. Sven will take carved soapstone to sell when he goes trading down the coast.

OUTCROP OF SOAPSTONE

A herdsman drives the Earl's cows to higher pasture away from the farm where there is plenty of good grass. The cows will stay there the whole summer and get fat.

RUBBISH HEAP

VEGETABLE GARDEN

Rollo, the Blacksmith, spends all day in his workshop with his assistant, Leif. Here they make pots and pans, farm tools and weapons out of iron.

THE LONG HOUSE

ROLLO GIVES ASTRID A NEW POT

ROLLO'S WORKSHOP

BATH HOUSE

WASHING CLOTHES

WOOL FROM THESE SHEEP WILL BE MADE INTO CLOTHES

Flax is growing in this field. Astrid will weave the flax into fine linen to make clothes for her family.

A freeman ploughs a field to get it ready for sowing a crop of barley.

WOODEN PLOUGH

4

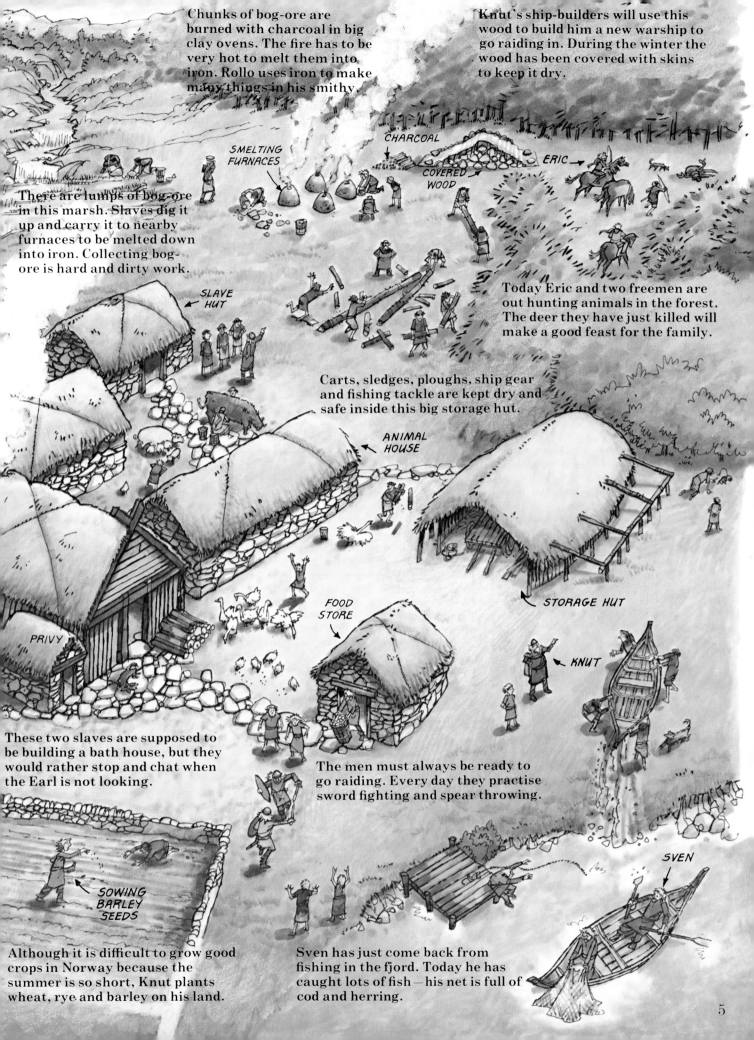

Chunks of bog-ore are burned with charcoal in big clay ovens. The fire has to be very hot to melt them into iron. Rollo uses iron to make many things in his smithy.

Knut's ship-builders will use this wood to build him a new warship to go raiding in. During the winter the wood has been covered with skins to keep it dry.

SMELTING FURNACES

CHARCOAL

COVERED WOOD

ERIC →

There are lumps of bog-ore in this marsh. Slaves dig it up and carry it to nearby furnaces to be melted down into iron. Collecting bog-ore is hard and dirty work.

SLAVE HUT

Today Eric and two freemen are out hunting animals in the forest. The deer they have just killed will make a good feast for the family.

Carts, sledges, ploughs, ship gear and fishing tackle are kept dry and safe inside this big storage hut.

ANIMAL HOUSE

STORAGE HUT

PRIVY

FOOD STORE

KNUT

These two slaves are supposed to be building a bath house, but they would rather stop and chat when the Earl is not looking.

The men must always be ready to go raiding. Every day they practise sword fighting and spear throwing.

SOWING BARLEY SEEDS

SVEN

Although it is difficult to grow good crops in Norway because the summer is so short, Knut plants wheat, rye and barley on his land.

Sven has just come back from fishing in the fjord. Today he has caught lots of fish — his net is full of cod and herring.

Inside the Longhouse

Earl Knut and his family live together in the longhouse. The one big room is always dark, smoky and a bit smelly as there are no windows. A small hole in the roof lets out the smoke.

While he waits for his morning meal, the Earl is carving arrows. Astrid is weaving the last length of wool for the sail of his new ship. Eric is already out working on the farm.

At one end of the room, the women are busy preparing and cooking the food. Today, the family will eat hot barley and oat porridge, bread rolls, butter, cheese and milk.

Only Knut and Astrid have a proper bed to sleep in — everybody else lies on platforms. Knut's slaves sleep huddled together on the floor of their hut to keep warm.

There is very little furniture. The family keep all their things in big wooden chests.

BJÖRN

METAL OIL LAMP

WOODEN CHEST

SLAVE

SOUR MILK

How to Make Bread

1 QUERN
FLOUR
HOLE TO PUT IN GRAIN

The bread-maker grinds barley grain in a big quern made of stone. She turns the handle until the grain is ground into flour.

2 KNEADING DOUGH

Then she mixes the flour with water and kneads it together in a big wooden trough to make a dough.

3 METAL PAN

When the dough is properly mixed, the bread-maker shapes it into small loaves and bakes them over the hot ashes of the fire.

FLOUR

SOAPSTONE OIL LAMP

Making Wool into Thread

1 In early summer, Sven cuts the wool off the sheep with big, metal shears. Freyda washes the fleece in a stream and then hangs it up to dry.

2 To get rid of the knots and burrs, Freyda combs the wool over and over again with long metal-pronged combs. Now the wool is ready to be spun.

METAL COMB

3 She ties some wool to a stick. Then she spins the spindle and lets it drop. As it falls, still spinning, she pulls out more wool to make a thread.

STICK CALLED DISTAFF

SPINDLE

SOAPSTONE WEIGHT

4 Freyda takes the thread off the spindle and winds it round a yarn-winder. Sometimes she dyes the thread different colours with vegetable juices.

DYED THREAD

Eric's wife is beating flax to break it into short, thin threads. When she has enough, she will spin them into a long thread and give it to Astrid to weave into linen.

Freyda is very pleased with the ironing board Björn has made for her. He carved it out of whalebone. She smooths the clothes with a big, heated lump of glass.

The girls learn how to spin and weave when they are quite young. Astrid spends hours each day at her loom. From the cloth she weaves, she makes clothes, ship sails, blankets and wall hangings.

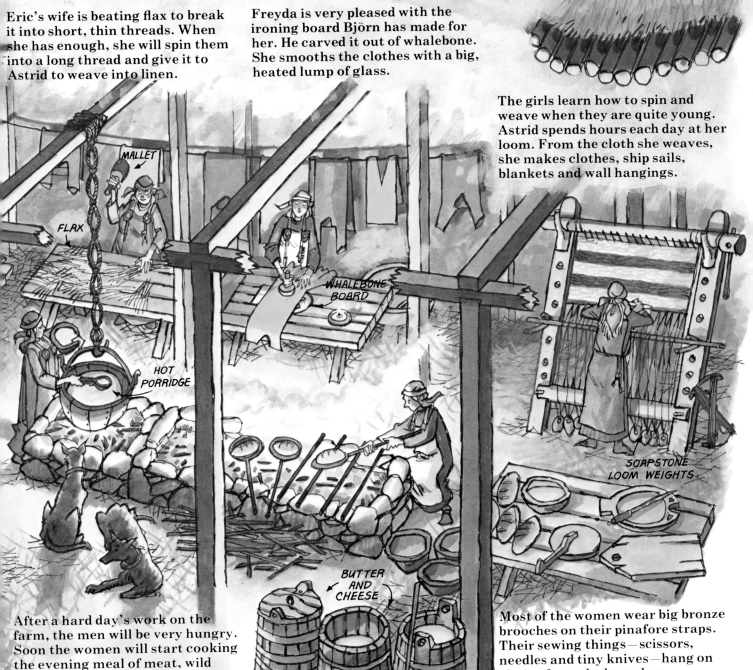

MALLET

FLAX

WHALEBONE BOARD

HOT PORRIDGE

SOAPSTONE LOOM WEIGHTS

BUTTER AND CHEESE

After a hard day's work on the farm, the men will be very hungry. Soon the women will start cooking the evening meal of meat, wild vegetables and fruit.

Most of the women wear big bronze brooches on their pinafore straps. Their sewing things—scissors, needles and tiny knives—hang on chains from the brooches.

Building a New Warship

For many weeks Earl Knut's freemen have been hard at work building a new warship. Carefully chosen trees from the forest were felled and left to dry long before the work began.

Knut has come to watch the carpenters rivet on the final planks—his ship is nearly ready. Soon he and his warriors will set off in the ship to spend the summer raiding.

The warship must be big and strong enough to cross the rough open sea to Ireland. It is about 24 metres long and 5 metres wide. There is room for 40 men to live on board.

Carpenters use adzes to shape a long, thick mast. The mast slots into a huge block of wood, shaped like a fish, in the middle of the warship's deck.

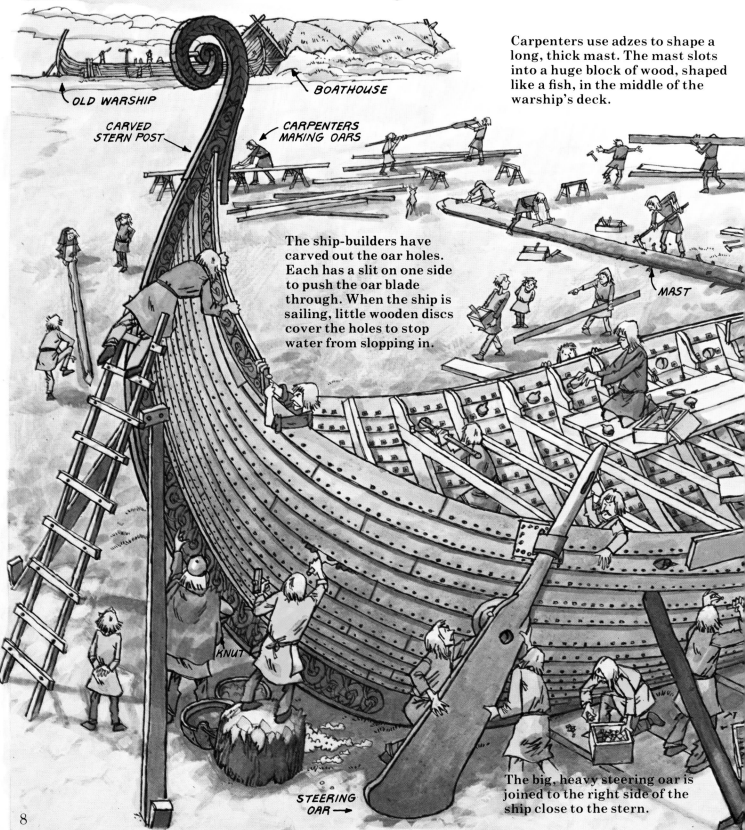

OLD WARSHIP

CARVED STERN POST

BOATHOUSE

CARPENTERS MAKING OARS

The ship-builders have carved out the oar holes. Each has a slit on one side to push the oar blade through. When the ship is sailing, little wooden discs cover the holes to stop water from slopping in.

MAST

KNUT

STEERING OAR →

The big, heavy steering oar is joined to the right side of the ship close to the stern.

How a Ship is Built

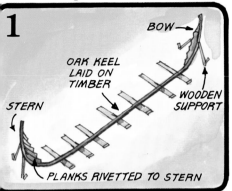

1

BOW

OAK KEEL
LAID ON
TIMBER

STERN

WOODEN
SUPPORT

PLANKS RIVETTED TO STERN

The trunk of a very tall oak tree is cut and shaped to make a strong, heavy keel. A curved piece of wood is joined to the front to make the bow. A second piece is joined to the back to make the stern.

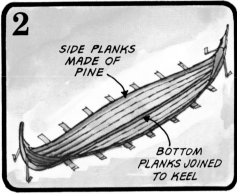

2

SIDE PLANKS
MADE OF
PINE

BOTTOM
PLANKS JOINED
TO KEEL

The carpenters cut long planks out of pine trees. The pine planks, which make the ship light, are rivetted to the keel, bow and stern to form the bottom and the sides of the ship.

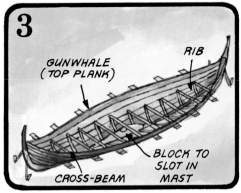

3

GUNWHALE
(TOP PLANK)

RIB

CROSS-BEAM

BLOCK TO
SLOT IN
MAST

Then the ribs and cross-beams are fitted inside the ship. The planks are tied or rivetted to them. A huge block of wood is fixed into the bottom of the ship to hold up the heavy mast.

Most of the floorboards are nailed down. A few are left loose so that they can be lifted up, when the ship is at sea, to bail water out of the bottom. Spare oars and other ship gear are stored under the deck.

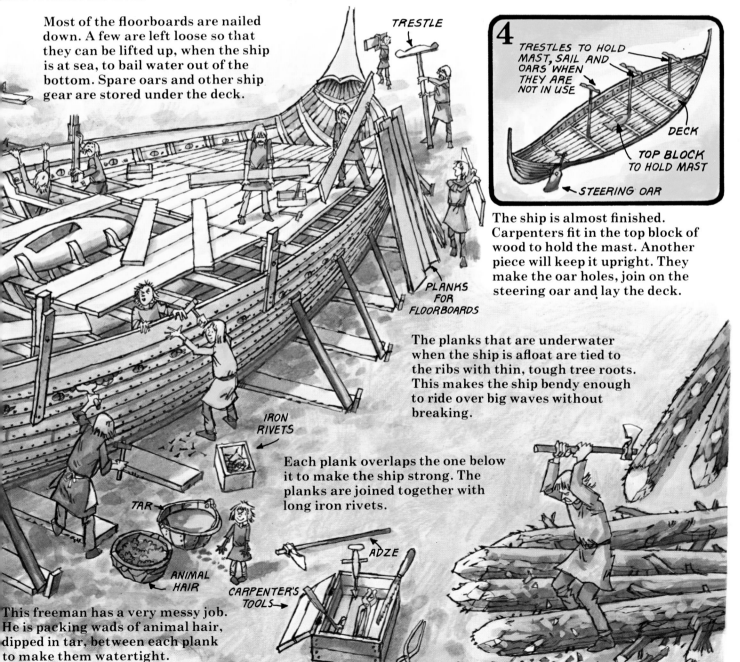

TRESTLE

PLANKS
FOR
FLOORBOARDS

IRON
RIVETS

TAR

ANIMAL
HAIR

ADZE

CARPENTER'S
TOOLS

4

TRESTLES TO HOLD
MAST, SAIL AND
OARS WHEN
THEY ARE
NOT IN USE

DECK

TOP BLOCK
TO HOLD MAST

STEERING OAR

The ship is almost finished. Carpenters fit in the top block of wood to hold the mast. Another piece will keep it upright. They make the oar holes, join on the steering oar and lay the deck.

The planks that are underwater when the ship is afloat are tied to the ribs with thin, tough tree roots. This makes the ship bendy enough to ride over big waves without breaking.

Each plank overlaps the one below it to make the ship strong. The planks are joined together with long iron rivets.

This freeman has a very messy job. He is packing wads of animal hair, dipped in tar, between each plank to make them watertight.

The Raiders Get Ready

At last Earl Knut's new ship is finished. Now he can go raiding. His three sons, Eric, Sven and Björn, and his most trusted freemen will go with him.

While they are away, the farm work must be done. Astrid is staying behind with five freemen and the slaves to help look after the farm.

Olaf, the Earl's cousin, has sailed down the coast to join him on the raids. Two other great chieftains and their warriors are going as well.

The Blacksmith's Workshop

THRUSTING SPEARS

BATTLE AXES

LEIF

THROWING SPEARS

CHARCOAL

METAL HELMETS

ROLLO

IRON ARROW HEADS

IRON ORE

RAIDERS' SWORDS

ANVIL

RIVETS

TONGS

Rollo is making and mending weapons for the raiders. His helper, Leif, keeps the charcoal fire glowing with big bellows. It makes him hot and bad-tempered.

When an iron bar is red hot, Rollo takes it off the fire with his tongs and beats it into shape on the anvil. He is making an axe as a present for Cousin Olaf.

Rollo decorates the axes, spears and swords he makes for chieftains with gold and silver. He may spend as long as a month working on a really special weapon.

Fighting Practice

THROWING SPEARS

WRESTLERS

ARCHERS

BJÖRN

EARL KNUT IN HIS CHAIN MAIL SHIRT

THRUSTING SPEARS

The Vikings are very proud of being good fighters and owning fine weapons. Even young boys learn how to fight. Today is the last time for Knut and his men to practise before going on the raids.

Each man owns a sword, a spear, an axe and a shield—a few have bows and arrows. Some warriors have throwing spears which they hurl at the enemy, others have ones specially made for thrusting.

A Viking raider's most precious possession is his sword. With its sharp edges, it is a deadly weapon. Only great men, such as Knut and Olaf, wear coats of mail and metal helmets in battle.

Loading up the Ship

Everybody helps to load up the new warship. The raiders take with them all the things they will need for the long voyage ahead. But very little food is carried aboard— only a few barrels of fresh water and sour milk, some flour and bags of dried fish and meat.

Knut and his men will steal what food they need from the villages they raid. They are hoping to find many rich monasteries to rob of their goods and treasures. Between raids, the warriors will camp on shore. But they must stay close to their ships in case they are attacked and have to make a quick get-away. Only Knut has a tent and a proper bed to sleep on. His men must make do with skin sleeping bags and the hard ground.

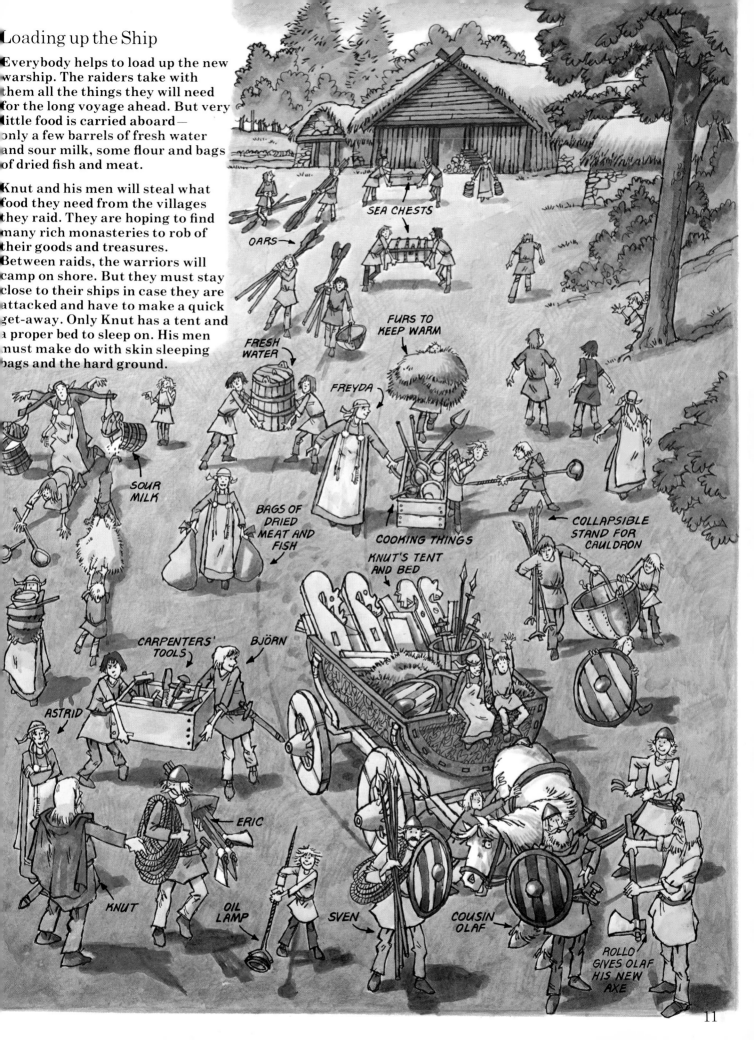

SEA CHESTS

OARS →

FRESH WATER

FURS TO KEEP WARM

FREYDA

SOUR MILK

BAGS OF DRIED MEAT AND FISH

COOKING THINGS

COLLAPSIBLE STAND FOR CAULDRON

KNUT'S TENT AND BED

CARPENTERS' TOOLS

BJÖRN

ASTRID

ERIC

KNUT

OIL LAMP

SVEN

COUSIN OLAF

ROLLO GIVES OLAF HIS NEW AXE

Setting Off

At dawn the next day, the chieftains and their warriors begin the long, hard voyage to Ireland. It is a good day for sailing, with a clear sky and a strong wind behind them.

Knut is excited about spending the summer raiding. But Astrid and the other women are sad to see their men go—some may not return. They may be killed in battle or drowned at sea.

The raiders will spend several days living and sleeping on their ships out of sight of land. It is very cramped on board and they will have an uncomfortable journey with little to do.

COUSIN OLAF

STEERING OAR

Cousin Olaf is helmsman on his ship. As the men row, he guides it down the fjord past dangerous rocks near the shore. By moving the tiller on the steering oar, Olaf can make the ship go left or right. In shallow water, he lifts it clear of the bottom. Each rower sits on a big, wooden chest, packed with his belongings.

FREYDA

Life on Board

Ship life is very boring when the weather is calm and the wind is blowing in the right direction. There is nothing to do but eat, sleep and fish. At night the men sleep on deck in bags made of skin. They take turns to keep watch for land and sleep during the day.

KNUT SAYS GOODBYE TO ASTRID

On this warship the crew now raise the mast and hoist the sail. It is very tricky and heavy work—the mast is long and weighs over 300 kilos. Most of the oars have been pulled in, but a few of the men keep theirs in the water to steady the ship as the mast goes up.

If possible, the Vikings sail along the coasts. But when they sail out of sight of land, they use the sun, the North Star and a kind of compass to help them go in the right direction. Coastal birds show them that land is near.

Sailing out of the fjord, the leading ship heads for the open sea. Its big, square sail is lashed to a long pole called the yard-arm which can be turned to catch the wind. The crew use the ropes at the bottom corners of the sail to control it.

SEALS

OARS

TILLER

ERIC

LOG BEING CARRIED TO FRONT OF SHIP

Eric is in charge of his father's new warship. Slaves help him and the crew to push it into the water. As the ship moves slowly over the logs, the men pick up those at the back and lay them in front of the ship.

13

Raiding a Monastery

For two days now the raiders have been in Ireland. After one successful raid on a village, they have found a rich monastery to rob of its precious treasures. The younger warriors hope to win fame by fighting bravely, seizing riches and capturing prisoners to take home.

When they saw the Viking warships, the terrified people from nearby farms fled to the walled monastery for safety. They sent a runner off to fetch help. A few men armed themselves with hunting spears and woodmen's axes. The monks hurried into the church and prayed to God to save them from the pagan warriors.

The raiders set fire to the houses to force out the people. Their attack must be quick and they must leave before news of their arrival spreads. As soon as they have seized enough treasure and prisoners, they will sail down the coast to set up camp. There they will share out the loot, dress their wounds, mend their weapons and get ready for another raid.

NOBLEMAN'S FORT

A party of warriors ride off on stolen horses to raid a nearby nobleman's house.

A herdsman tries to drive his sheep away to save them from the raiders.

Young monks rush from the burning schoolhouse where they have their daily lessons.

SCHOOL HOUSE

HERDSMAN

Knut has snatched the treasure from the church. The gold altar cross and gospel book will fetch a good price in Norway. He will give the casket to Astrid as a present.

YOUNG MONKS

BJÖRN

KNUT

MONKS

SVEN

ERIC

Eric and Sven have found a hoard of hidden treasure. When he next goes trading, Sven will sell the silver plates. The coins can be made into fine jewellery.

14

Irish horsemen attack the Vikings who have been left to guard the ships. Until help arrives, the raiders link their shields together to defend themselves. Cousin Olaf has been badly wounded by an Irish arrow.

IRISH HORSEMEN

COUSIN OLAF

Some raiders slaughter cows and sheep to take back to the camp for roasting. Three others have gone off in search of bread and honey.

A chieftain counts the prisoners herded together against the monastery wall. The abbot will only be released if the Irish pay a ransom to the raiders of a bag of silver. The others will be sold as slaves in Norway.

GRAVE STONE

ARMED VILLAGERS

CHIEFTAIN

THE ABBOT

Three villagers do their best to fight off the attack, killing one Viking with their hunting spears.

A MONK'S HOUSE

Women and children are rounded up by the raiders. They will be taken as slaves. A few lucky ones manage to escape.

15

A Big Feast

At the end of the summer, Knut and his warriors sailed back to Norway. Their ship was loaded with goods and prisoners from many successful raids.

Astrid has prepared a huge feast to celebrate the raiders' victories. For days, she and the women have worked hard cooking a splendid meal. For such a special occasion, cows and sheep have been slaughtered to roast on spits. And deer and wild boars have been hunted in the forest.

Knut invited the other chieftains to the feast. But Cousin Olaf has been taken home. He is gravely ill and Knut fears he may die.

Everyone wears their best clothes and jewellery for the feast. The longhouse rings with their laughter and songs. Each raider brags of his bravery and cunning against the enemy. Long into the night, they drink and talk, telling stories of storms at sea, and the strange land and people they have seen.

WINNER OF THE DRINKING CONTEST

HORN

ASTRID'S SPECIALLY BREWED BEER

SLICES OF BEEF

COOK BRAISING WILD BOAR STEAKS

ROAST SHEEP

GAMING BOARD

ERIC

Everyone gets very dirty eating with their fingers, but some guests have knives or wooden spoons. They drink from carved cow horns, glasses or wooden cups.

Astrid's Jewellery

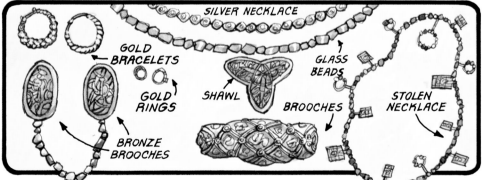

SILVER NECKLACE

GOLD BRACELETS

GOLD RINGS

SHAWL

GLASS BEADS

BROOCHES

STOLEN NECKLACE

BRONZE BROOCHES

Rollo, the blacksmith, has made many fine pieces of jewellery for Astrid. Over the hot charcoals of his fire, he melts down gold coins and silver bowls.

Then he works the precious metals into brooches, necklaces, rings and bracelets. Knut has stolen jewellery on his raids and brought it back for Astrid to wear.

Astrid's Jewel Box

This is Astrid's new jewel box. The words the rune master has carved on it say 'Astridr a Kistu Thasa' which means 'Astrid owns this casket'.

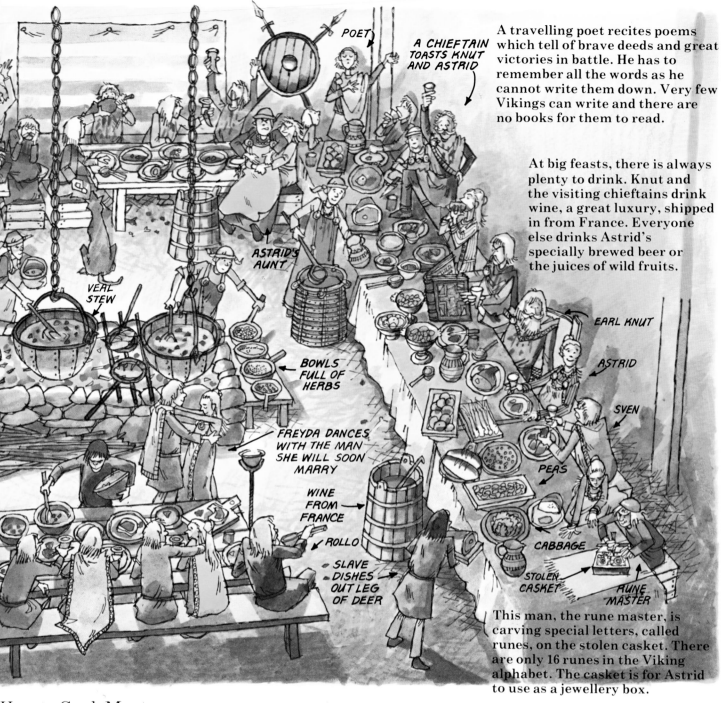

POET

A CHIEFTAIN TOASTS KNUT AND ASTRID

A travelling poet recites poems which tell of brave deeds and great victories in battle. He has to remember all the words as he cannot write them down. Very few Vikings can write and there are no books for them to read.

At big feasts, there is always plenty to drink. Knut and the visiting chieftains drink wine, a great luxury, shipped in from France. Everyone else drinks Astrid's specially brewed beer or the juices of wild fruits.

VEAL STEW

ASTRID'S AUNT

BOWLS FULL OF HERBS

EARL KNUT

ASTRID

SVEN

FREYDA DANCES WITH THE MAN SHE WILL SOON MARRY

PEAS

WINE FROM FRANCE

ROLLO

CABBAGE

SLAVE DISHES OUT LEG OF DEER

STOLEN CASKET

RUNE MASTER

This man, the rune master, is carving special letters, called runes, on the stolen casket. There are only 16 runes in the Viking alphabet. The casket is for Astrid to use as a jewellery box.

How to Cook Meat

Spit-Roasted

First a slave cuts off the head and feet of a dead animal and takes out its insides. Then he roasts the meat over the fire on a long, iron rod.

Baked

HOT STONES

MEAT

Sometimes meat is baked in a big hole in the ground. Hot stones are packed round the meat and it is covered with earth until it is cooked.

1 Boiled

WOOD LINED PIT

HERBS

This way of cooking meat takes a long time. A wood-lined pit is filled with water and chunks of meat are put into it. To make it more tasty, the

2

HOT STONES

cook adds herbs, such as cumin, juniper berries, mustard seeds and garlic. Then she drops hot stones from the fire into the pit to heat the water.

17

Cousin Olaf Dies

Cousin Olaf is dying from his battle wounds. At his bedside, Knut and Astrid pray to the Viking gods to help save the famous chieftain's life.

They believe that their gods are magnificent heroes, who can perform great feats of magic and strength and who are powerful, fearless warriors.

The family beg Thor, god of thunder, and Odin, chief of the gods, to answer their prayers. Without their help and powers, Olaf Strongarm will die.

1 At Olaf's Bedside

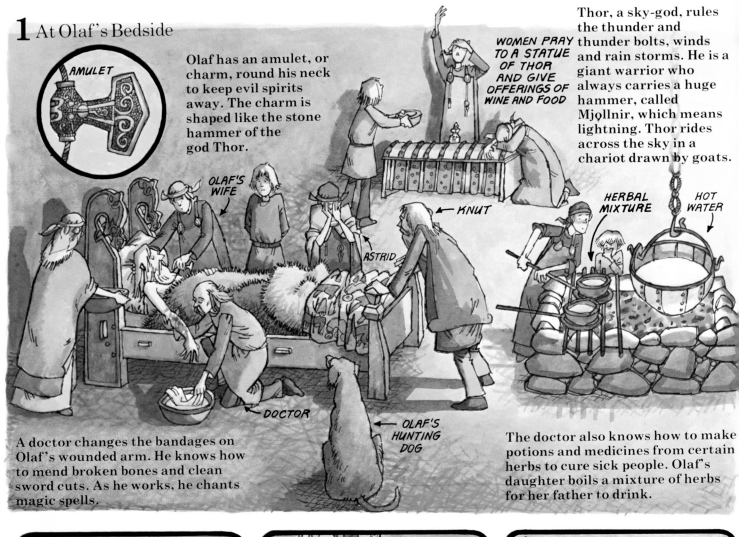

AMULET

Olaf has an amulet, or charm, round his neck to keep evil spirits away. The charm is shaped like the stone hammer of the god Thor.

WOMEN PRAY TO A STATUE OF THOR AND GIVE OFFERINGS OF WINE AND FOOD

OLAF'S WIFE

KNUT

ASTRID

HERBAL MIXTURE

HOT WATER

DOCTOR

OLAF'S HUNTING DOG

Thor, a sky-god, rules the thunder and thunder bolts, winds and rain storms. He is a giant warrior who always carries a huge hammer, called Mjǫllnir, which means lightning. Thor rides across the sky in a chariot drawn by goats.

A doctor changes the bandages on Olaf's wounded arm. He knows how to mend broken bones and clean sword cuts. As he works, he chants magic spells.

The doctor also knows how to make potions and medicines from certain herbs to cure sick people. Olaf's daughter boils a mixture of herbs for her father to drink.

2 Prayers and medicine did not save Olaf's life. His grief-stricken wife prepares his body for burial. Olaf will be buried in his best clothes and finest jewellery.

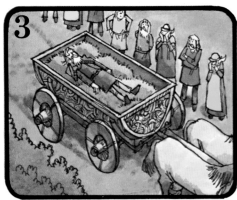

3 Olaf's body is carried to the family cemetery in a horse-drawn wagon. His father, also a great chieftain, and his mother were buried there when they died.

4 Two of Olaf's finest horses and his faithful hunting dog are led away to be killed. By some magic, the people believe, they will live again with Olaf in his after-life.

5 The Burial

EARTH TO FILL IN GRAVE

THE GRAVE OF OLAF'S FATHER

THE GRAVE OF OLAF'S MOTHER

Because he was such a famous and wealthy man, Cousin Olaf is buried with his warship. A special wooden chamber has been built on the deck for him to lie in.

The Vikings believe that Olaf will sail in his ship to another world. His most treasured and useful possessions are buried with him to help him in this life-after-death.

He will probably live in Valhalla—the Viking heaven. Here the god Odin has a splendid hall for the dead. Only the bravest and greatest warriors go to Valhalla.

How Other Vikings are Buried

Poor Person's Grave

Poor people are buried in a big hole in the ground with a few of their belongings. This Viking woman has two spindles, a comb and a barrel of milk at her side.

Funeral Pyre

Sometimes dead Viking warriors are burnt on a pile of wood called a pyre. Their swords are bent, their spears broken and shields slashed and thrown on the fire with them.

Slave Dies with Master

This slave was killed to be buried with her master. Very few slaves die like this. Because he was a rich farmer, her master has a wood-lined grave.

Björn Sails to Iceland

The following spring, Björn plans to take his family to live in Iceland. Some freemen and a few slaves are going with him to help build a house and work on the land.

In Norway, most of the good land is already being farmed. There is little left for young farmers and their families. Many have left to settle and farm in other countries.

It will take Björn several weeks to reach Iceland. He will sail in the new ship his father has given him. It has a big hold in the deck to carry all the cargo Björn is taking with him.

1 Getting Ready to Leave

BJÖRN

WEAVING LOOM

BARLEY SEED

SLEDGE

SOUR MILK AND FRESH WATER

PLOUGH

As well as household things, clothes and camping gear, Björn loads animals into the ship for breeding in Iceland. He is taking his plough, food for the animals and bags of barley seed to plant.

2 Visiting Friends in the Shetlands

BJÖRN'S SHIP

RUBBISH

SHETLAND PONIES

On the way to Iceland, Björn visits some Viking friends who live on one of the tiny Shetland Islands. Their life here is more peaceful than it was in Norway. They grow barley and vegetables and keep sheep and cows. When the sea is calm, men fish for cod.

3 Shipwrecked on the Faroes

Björn and his family stay with their friends for a few days before sailing on. After four calm days at sea, they are caught in a bad storm near the rocky coast of the Faroe Islands.

Björn struggles to keep his ship away from the islands but it is blown on to jagged rocks. Although it is battered by the waves and holed on one side, he and his crew manage to row the ship ashore.

4 Repairing the Ship

Safe on the shore, the friendly islanders help Björn to repair his ship. They left Norway six years ago to settle here. They tell Björn more about Iceland and say there is still plenty of good farming land for new settlers.

5 Arriving in Iceland

When the ship is ready, Björn sets off once again. After many days at sea, he sees Iceland on the horizon. It is a strange island, with plumes of smoke and steam from volcanoes, and jagged, treeless mountains topped with snow.

As he sails round the south coast of the island, Björn finds that all the flat land has already been settled. But further west, he discovers some unclaimed land that looks good for farming. The soil is rich and there is plenty of grass for his animals.

SEALS

GEYSERS

BJÖRN'S LAND

GLACIER

FISHERMEN

SETTLED LAND

BJÖRN'S SHIP

Sven Goes Trading

In autumn, after another summer of raiding, Sven takes his wife down the coast to the big trading town of Hedeby. With his share of the loot—six young, healthy slaves and a bag of silver, Sven hopes to buy silk cloth and other costly things that come from foreign countries. Knut has also given him some soapstone bowls from the farm to sell.

Hedeby is a very exciting place. Today it is full of Viking merchants, busy exchanging their goods.

A few Arab traders have travelled overland from Asia to sell silk and buy slaves to take back home. As the Viking men trade, they joke and tell stories of their recent raids. The women stop to hear the latest gossip and to stare at the strange foreigners.

In many parts of the town, craftsmen are hard at work—making combs, skin shoes and woollen cloth to trade with. Clay pots, amber beads, farm tools, ropes and weapons are on sale as well.

PALISADE TO HARBOUR SHIPS AND KEEP OUT ENEMIES

TRADING SHIPS

FISH

GUARD KEEPS WATCH FOR INVADERS

Sven Buys Wine and Silk

ARAB TRADER SELLING SILK

SVEN

SOAPSTONE BOWLS

BARREL OF WINE

In mid-winter, there will be a festival on Knut's farm. Sven buys wine and drinking glasses for the feast. In exchange, he gives the trader three Irish slaves and silver arm bands. The silver is weighed on scales.

Vikings weigh silver to find out how much it is worth. Arm and neck bands are worth the same as equal weights of coins. Later on, Sven will sell three more slaves and some soapstone bowls to buy silk for his wife.

Most of the houses in Hedeby are made of wattle and daub (sticks woven together and packed with mud). Some are made from split tree trunks. The reed-thatched roofs have a hole in the gables to let out the smoke from the fire.

VISITING MERCHANTS
SET UP CAMP

WALL OF EARTH AND WOOD
TO STOP INVADERS

BURIAL GROUND

WELL

HOUSE MADE OF SPLIT LOGS

MAIN STREET

SLAVES

SVEN AND WIFE

FISH ON SALE

CLAY POTS

WEAVER

SHOE MAKER

AMBER BEADS

ANIMAL SACRIFICE TO THE GODS

WATTLE AND DAUB HOUSE

COMB MAKERS

SELLING VENISON

1 Making Combs

COMB-MAKER

The craftsman makes his combs out of deer antlers. First he cuts the points off the antler and shaves down the rough outside.

2 STRIP FOR HANDLE OF COMB

PLATES OF ANTLER FOR TEETH

Then the comb-maker carves a smooth, flat strip to make the top of the comb, and cuts small plates for the teeth.

3 PLATES RIVETTED TO HANDLE AND CUT INTO TEETH

He rivets the plates to the top and then cuts them up into fine teeth. Then he decorates the comb with carvings.

4 COMB CASES

SPOONS

Craftsmen also make comb cases, spoons, spindles and handles for knives out of bone. They sell them to the traders.

23

Björn Settles in Iceland

Björn and his family have been in Iceland for almost three months. At first they camped while the freemen and slaves built a farmhouse. Now they have all moved in to it.

Autumn in Iceland is a busy time for farmers. Some settlers, who live nearby, have come to help Björn get things ready before the winter begins. They cut the long grass to make into hay, and rake up the fallen leaves. Björn's animals will need a lot of food if they are to live through the long, cold winter.

All summer, his sheep, cows and goats have been grazing in the meadows. Now they must be herded together and driven down to the farm for shelter. Sturdy goats may be let out to graze, but it will be too cold for sheep and cows.

Björn's wife is worried that the family may not have enough food for the winter. She guts fish to dry on racks in the wind. The meat from slaughtered animals is pickled, salted and packed into barrels.

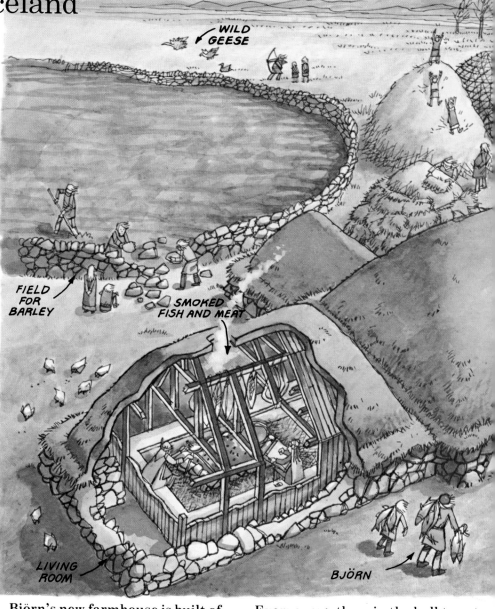

WILD GEESE

FIELD FOR BARLEY

SMOKED FISH AND MEAT

LIVING ROOM

BJÖRN

Björn's new farmhouse is built of driftwood washed up on the beach, and cartloads of heavy stones. Thick blocks of turf cover the roof to keep out the cold.

Everyone gathers in the hall to eat, work and chat. Earth is packed into platforms along the walls for them to sit and sleep on. There is also a big living room.

Work in Iceland

1 Salting Meat

CAULDRON OF SEAWATER

Big cauldrons filled with seawater and seaweed are boiled over a wood fire. When all the water boils away, crystals of salt are left on the bottom of the pots.

2

DEAD COW

CRYSTALS OF SALT

One woman scrapes the crystals from the pots, another chops up a dead cow. To stop the meat from going bad, strips are packed in barrels with the salt.

Drying Meat and Fish

While Björn's wife dries chunks of meat and gutted cod, a freeman teaches his son how to light a fire of moss and twigs. He strikes a hard stone against some iron to make the first spark.

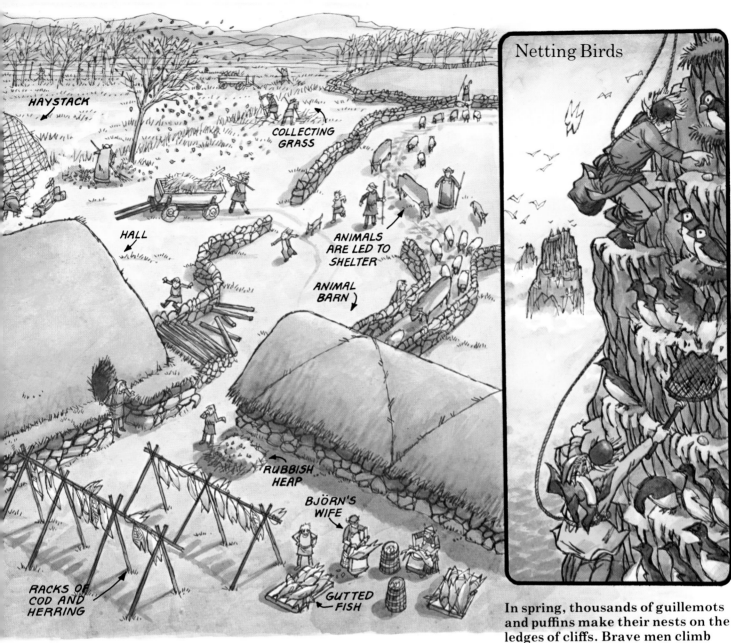

HAYSTACK

COLLECTING GRASS

HALL

ANIMALS ARE LED TO SHELTER

ANIMAL BARN

RUBBISH HEAP

BJÖRN'S WIFE

GUTTED FISH

RACKS OF COD AND HERRING

Netting Birds

In spring, thousands of guillemots and puffins make their nests on the ledges of cliffs. Brave men climb carefully up the dangerous rocks to trap the birds in big nets. Today the climb has been successful. The men have caught many birds to eat.

Here the women sit close to the hearth to do their work. They will spend most of the winter spinning and weaving, feeding the animals and looking after the children.

When the winter is over, Björn will plough his field and plant a crop of barley. The family will help him dig up peat and chop up wood for fuel for the summer.

Catching a Whale

Björn spotted this small whale while he was out fishing. He and his crew drive it into shallow water to kill it. The whale blubber will be melted down for oil. The meat is good for eating.

Hunting Seals

Two hunters creep up on seals basking in the sun. They will spear as many as they can before the seals slip back into the sea. Vikings make ropes and shoes from sealskin and eat seal meat.

Collecting Feathers

An eider duck makes her nest on the ground. She plucks down from her breast to line the nest. Two women collect some of the down to fill pillows and bed covers. They also steal some tasty eider eggs.

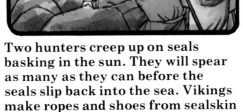

25

A Meeting of the Thing

Earl Knut and other freemen from this area of Norway have come to attend a big meeting. This gathering of freemen, which happens a few times a year, is called the Thing.

The men are here to discuss important local business matters, and to decide what to do with three criminals. Some have brought their wives to join in the discussions.

Everyone has set up camp nearby as the Thing will probably last for many days. It is a good opportunity for sports and gossip, and for tinkers to do a bit of trading.

Two criminals are led away to be punished. The man, a thief, is to have one hand cut off. The woman, found guilty of being a witch, will be stoned or drowned.

STALLION

TINKERS

WITCH   THIEF   ROLLO'S WIFE   ROLLO'S SON   LEIF   LAW SPEAKER   EARL KNUT

Knut and Astrid are particularly interested in the meeting. Leif, their apprentice blacksmith, is accused of murdering his master, Rollo, in a fit of rage. Now it will be decided if he is guilty.

The Earl and four local chieftains have been chosen to head the meeting. One of them, the law speaker, recites the law to the crowd. Together they must all agree on Leif's punishment.

Leif, a very stubborn man, refuses to answer any questions. The crowd find him guilty of murder. As a punishment, he is banished from the land. Leif must go at once before Rollo's family kill him.

Weight Lifting

Vikings love to show off their great strength. One of their favourite games is to see who can lift the heaviest boulder. This man is delighted—he has just won the boulder-lifting competition.

Wrestling

Wrestling is also a popular sport. Each day, after the freemen have ended their talks, the toughest Vikings compete against each other to see who is the best and strongest wrestler.

Stallion Fighting

Fierce, wild stallions—specially bred for fighting—have been brought to the Thing. Sometimes, during a horse-fight, the owners get so excited, they start to fight with each other.

A Winter Festival

Tonight, Knut and Astrid have asked all their friends to a festival at the farm. They hold one every winter. Astrid is known throughout the district for her good parties and her delicious food.

The family are very excited. It is always great fun at the feast, with poets and ballad singers, dancing and drinking to entertain the guests.

There is much to do before everyone arrives. Astrid and Freyda prepare the food and drink. Sven collects wood for the hearth. The children are just a nuisance—they much prefer play to work.

WOOD FOR HEARTH

SVEN

STORE HOUSE

ASTRID

KNUT

DRIED MEAT AND FISH

FREYDA

SPECIALLY BREWED BEER

SNOW CLEARED OFF ICE

DEER

ERIC

WOODEN SKIS

BONE SKATES

Eric returns from a successful hunting trip. The four deer he has speared and the snared rabbits will be dished up at the feast tonight.

The Vikings' World

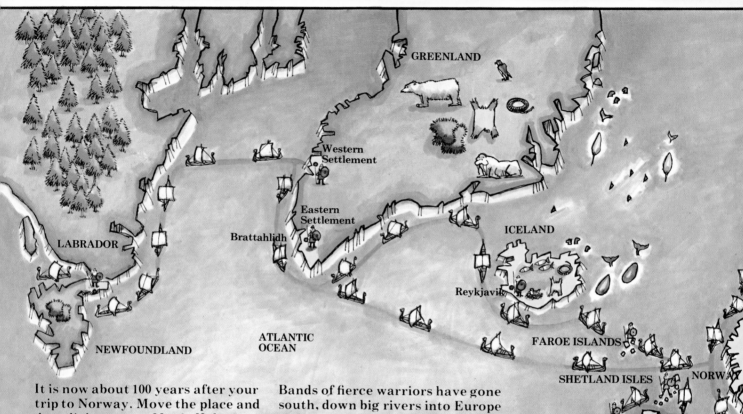

It is now about 100 years after your trip to Norway. Move the place and date dials on your Magic Helmet and look down on the world the Vikings have explored and invaded since then.

They have sailed from their homes in Scandinavia to raid and settle in many towns of Britain and Ireland. There, over the years, they have killed hundreds of people and carried others off as slaves.

Bands of fierce warriors have gone south, down big rivers into Europe and even as far as North Africa to steal, kill and trade. In Central Asia, they have met Arabs, with their long caravans of camels, coming back from China with fine silk and other rare things to sell.

Many Norwegian Vikings have braved the open sea and sailed west to explore and settle in Iceland, Greenland and America.

What the Vikings Found

timber	weapons	jewels	pottery	falcons	Arabs
furs	feathers	wheat	glass	spices	Slavs
walrus ivory	soap-stone	tin	gold	sword blades	Vikings
hides	cloth	honey	amber	Viking overland routes	Franks
ropes	slaves	salt	silver	Viking river routes	caravan routes
fish	loot	wine	silk	Viking sea routes	trading towns

As great warriors, adventurers, traders and settlers the Vikings have travelled to many parts of the world. This map shows you the ways they went, all the places they have visited, the people they have met and the things they have found on their travels.

ARCTIC OCEAN

Tashkent

Samarkand

Bulgar

ARAL SEA

Bokhara

Staraja Lagoda

Novgorod

CASPIAN SEA

Birka

Gnezdovo

Grobina

SWEDEN

R. Volga

Gurgan

Wiskiauten

Kiev

Truso

Wolin

R. Dneiper

Elbe

Cracow

Prague

BLACK SEA

R. Tigris

R. Danube

Baghdad

Constantinople

R. Euphrates

PERSIAN GULF

ITALY

Rome

Sidon

SARDINIA

Jerusalem

CRETE

CYPRUS

SICILY

Alexandria

MEDITERRANEAN SEA

NORTH AFRICA

The Story of the Vikings

The first Viking raids began in about 793 A.D. when a band of Viking warriors attacked the monastery on Lindisfarne, a small island on the north-east coast of Britain. There they murdered many people and captured others. News of this attack spread terror all over Europe. Many Christian people there had already heard of these fierce men from the North.

A year later, the raiders came back to England and attacked monasteries at Monkwearmouth and Jarrow. In 795 A.D., Vikings from Norway began raiding Ireland, killing and looting everywhere they went. About this time, a few Norwegian Vikings settled on the Scottish islands, and on the Isle of Man.

Other bands of Viking raiders sailed in their warships along the coasts of Germany, France, Spain, Italy and North Africa. There they stole whatever riches they could find, again killing people and taking others as slaves.

Swedish Vikings went east to Russia, sailing down the great Volga and Dneiper rivers to raid and settle in towns such as Staraja Ladoga, Kiev, Novgorod and Gnezdovo.

At this time, the Vikings worshipped their own gods, like Thor, Odin and Frey. A missionary monk, called St. Ansgar, went to Birka in 830 to try to convert the people to Christianity. But he did not have much success. It was a long time before the Vikings became Christians.

From 835 A.D. onwards raids on England and Ireland became more and more frequent. Instead of making hit-and-run raids, as they had done before, the Northmen set up camps and stayed during the winter months. Then they began raiding again in the spring and summer. In 841, they settled for the first time in Ireland, at Dublin.

By now, many Vikings were leaving their homes to settle in other countries. In 860, Norwegian explorers discovered Iceland. The first Viking farmers settled there ten years later. By 930, about 10,000 Vikings were living there. The first Althing, a parliament, met and created a new Icelandic republic.

In 867, Danish raiders in England captured the city of York. Soon they had settled all over Northumbria. After years of battle between the Danes and the English, King Alfred of England signed a treaty with the Danish leader Guthrum. They divided the country between them. The Danish part of England was known as the Danelaw.

This treaty did not bring peace. The Vikings continued to raid the English coasts and King Alfred had to defend his land in many battles. It was not until 926, when Aethelstan was king, that the English recaptured Northumbria from the Danes. Aethelstan gathered a huge army and defeated them in a great battle.

Early in the 10th century, bands of Vikings sailed from Ireland to north-west England. They fought many battles, overpowering the people who lived there. Many Vikings also settled in northern Scotland. In Ireland – Dublin and Limerick became important trading ports.

In 911, Rollo, a Danish leader, took his warriors to Normandy in France. There they captured land from the Franks. Their leader, Charles the Simple, signed a treaty with Rollo making Normandy Viking territory.

It was not until about 930 that the Danish Vikings started to become Christians. Their king, Harald Bluetooth, was converted ten years later. In Norway, the people were forced to adopt the Christian religion. But many of them still continued to worship their own gods.

A Norwegian Viking, Eric the Red, who had been banished to Iceland for killing a man, heard of an unexplored island. In 982, he sailed from Iceland to live on this island which he called Greenland. A few years later he returned to Iceland with news of Greenland. Many people went back with him to live there.

In 1002, Erik's son, Leif Eriksson, sailed west from Greenland and found an island which he called 'Vinland'. This was probably Newfoundland. America had been discovered about 15 years before by a Viking explorer who had been blown off-course trying to get to Greenland. Some Vikings followed Leif to live in Vinland.

Early in the 11th century, the English were forced to pay money to the Vikings to make them leave their towns and people in peace. For several years the Vikings were given many pounds of silver to go away. This money was called Danegeld. But they kept returning until in 1016, Canute, king of Denmark, invaded and became king of England.

During this time, the Norwegian Vikings finally became Christians. They built churches to worship in and set up stones, called runestones, in memory of people who had died. The stones were carved with the runic alphabet (Viking alphabet) and many different patterns. But it was not until the 12th century that the Swedish Vikings finally became Christians.

Christianity changed the Vikings' way of life. They were not so fierce and no longer made many raids or demanded Danegeld. By 1066, the raids ceased and the Vikings settled down to a much quieter, more peaceful life. But they were still great traders and continued to trade in Britain and Ireland and all over Europe.

Wherever the Vikings settled they adopted the language and customs of the people there. They soon became French, English, Russian, Scots, or Irish themselves. Later, the people in Scandinavia, the Vikings' homeland, became Norwegians, Swedes and Danes. Even today, in the countries in which they settled, you can see the descendants of the tall, blond and blue-eyed Vikings.

Index

Amulet 18
Antler 23
Arab Trader 22–23

Bed 6, 11, 18
Blacksmith 4–5, 10
Bog-ore 5
Bread-maker 6

Camping 22–23, 26, 30
Camping equipment 11, 20
Cargo ship 20–21
Carpenters' tools 8–9, 11, 20
Comb-maker 23
Cooking 6–7, 16–17, 24–25
Cooking equipment 6–7, 11, 16–17, 20
Craftsmen 22–23
Crime 26
Criminal 26
Crops 4–5, 24–25

Danegeld 31
Danelaw 31
Deer 5, 27
Doctor 18
Drink,
  beer 16–17, 27
  fruit juice 16–17
  wine 17, 22

Eider down 25
Explorer 20–21, 30–31

Farm 4–5, 20, 24–25
  animal 4–5, 20, 24–25
  worker 4–5, 24–25
Faroe Islands 21
Feast 16–17, 27
Festival,
  winter 27
Fighting 5, 10, 14–15, 26
Fishing 5, 12
Fjord 5, 12–13
Flax 4, 7
Food 4–5, 6–7, 11, 15, 16–17, 20
  24–25, 27
Freemen 4–5, 8–9, 10, 20, 26
Funeral 18–19

Gods 18–19, 30–31
Grave 19, 23

Guillemot 25

Hedeby 22–23
House,
  animal 5
  bath 4
  foodstore 5, 27
  longhouse 4–5, 6–7, 16–17
  monk's 14–15
  slave hut 5
  smithy 4, 10
  turf 24–25
  wattle and daub 22–23
  wood 22–23
Hunting 5, 27

Iceland 21, 24–25
Ireland 14–15
Iron 5, 10

Jewellery 7, 16

Law 26
Law speaker 26
Linen 4, 7
Loot 14–15, 16–17, 30

Medicine 18
Merchant,
  Arab 22 23
  Viking 22 23
Monastery 14–15
Monk 14–15, 30

Norway 4–5, 16, 20, 26

Oil lamp,
  metal 6, 11, 16–17
  soapstone 6, 11

Plough 4–5, 20
Poet 17, 27
Prisoner 14–15
Puffin 25
Punishment 26

Raid 14–15
Rune master 17
Runes 16–17

Sailing 12–13, 20–21

Scales 22
Seal 25
Settler 20 21, 24 25, 30 31
Shetland Island 20
Ship,
  building 8 9
  cargo 20 21
  helmsman 12
  mast 8 9, 12 13
  sail 7, 13
  steering oar 8 9, 12
  trading 22
  war 8 9, 12 13, 14 15, 19, 30
Ship-builder 8 9
Silk 22
Skate 27
Ski 27
Slave 4 5, 6, 13, 19, 22 23, 30
Sledge 20, 27
Soapstone,
  for trade 4, 22
  loom weight 7
  oil lamp 6, 11
  spindle 7
Spinning 7, 25
  distaff 7
Stallion fighting 26

Thing (Meeting) 26
  Althing 30
Trader,
  Arab 22 23
  Viking 22 23, 31
Trading 22 23, 26, 28 29, 31
  town 22 23
  ship 22
Treasure 14 15, 16 17, 30 31

Wagon 11, 18
Warship 8 9, 12 13, 14 15, 19, 30
Weapon 10 11, 14 15
Weaving 7, 23, 25
  loom 7, 20
Weight lifting 26
Whale 25
Wood 5, 6, 8 9, 24, 27
Wool 4, 7
Wrestling 10, 26
Writing (runes) 17

Yarn-winder 7

Further Reading

Vikings and their Travels, Making History Series (Simon & Schuster, 1993)

Sail the Atlantic with the Vikings and Eric the Red, Beyond the Horizons Series (Evans Brothers, 1992)

The Vikings, Insight Series (Oxford, 1992).

The Vikings, History as Evidence Series (Kingfisher, 1992)

First published in 1977 by
Usborne Publishing Ltd
Usborne House
83-85 Saffron Hill
London EC1N 8RT
England

Copyright © 1993, 1990, 1977
Usborne Publishing Ltd.

Printed in Belgium UE

The Time Traveller Book of ROME AND ROMANS

Heather Amery and Patricia Vanags

Illustrated by Stephen Cartwright and Designed by John Jamieson

Contents

2   Going Back in Time

3   The People You Will Meet

4   On the Road to Rome

6   In the Streets of Rome

8   Petronius at Home

10   Going to School

12   Shops and Markets

14   Afternoon at the Baths

16   Gladiators and Charioteers

18   Building in the City

20   Petronius Gives a Feast

22   Summer in the Country

24   Marcus Joins the Army

26   Attacking a Citadel

28   The Roman Empire

30   The Story of Rome

32   Index and Further Reading

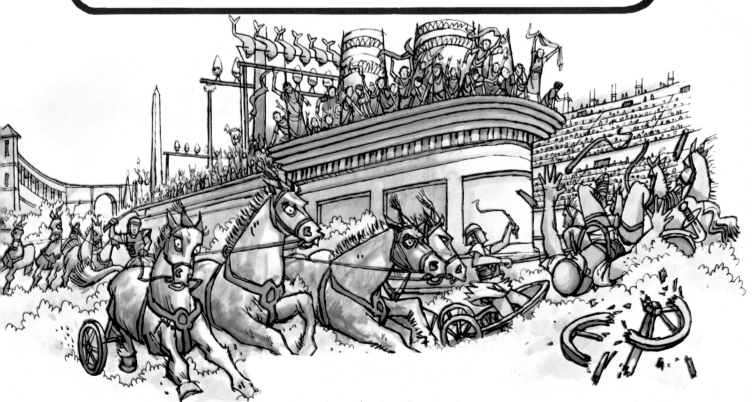

Going Back in Time

This is a book for everyone who would like to travel back in time. We have invented a Magic Time Travelling Helmet to help you. The trip to ancient Rome is nearly 2,000 years long but with the Helmet it takes seconds.

You may often have wanted to go to places you have read about in history; to see how people lived without all the things you know about—cars, television, telephones, jets and electric lights. In museums you

can see some of the odd things they used. But museums cannot show you it all in one place. Below you can see how the Helmet works and on the next page are the people you will meet when you are wearing it.

Put on the Helmet

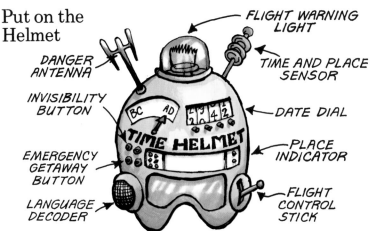

This is your Magic Time Travelling Helmet. You can see it has lots of useful buttons for

understanding foreign languages, for flying, for being invisible, and for a quick escape back to home.

Pick your Destination

This is where you are going. Set the 'Place' dial to 'Rome' and the 'Time' dial to 'A.D. 100'.

Below are a few stop-offs to give you an idea of how different things look when you jump back in time.

This is north-west Europe in 1940, before your parents were born.

Things have not changed very much but notice the aeroplane and old radio.

After a jump of 40 years, things have changed a lot. There is a gas lamp, no

electricity, a funny telephone and a lot of decorated furniture.

Back another 300 years and the room is lit by candles. Notice the small

window with little panes of glass. There is a big log fire in the fireplace.

Now we are at the time when people live in big, cold castles. There is

no chimney for the fire, nor glass in the windows. Next stop—ancient Rome.

The People You Will Meet

Everyone you will meet in this book lives in Rome. It is the capital of a great empire.

PETRONIUS

LIVIA

Petronius is a rich nobleman who lives in a large, comfortable house in Rome. He is a lawyer and an important official in the government. Petronius is a kind man who loves his wife, Livia, and his five children.

Cornelia, the eldest daughter, is 14 and is engaged to a young nobleman. Until her wedding, she lives at home, helping her mother in the house.

CORNELIA

CAIUS

Caius, the youngest, is eight and goes to school every day. He does not like the Greek schoolmaster and would rather play with his friends.

Pericles is secretary to Petronius. He is Greek and was a slave but he works so well, Petronius has given him his freedom and a special place in the household.

PERICLES

SHOPKEEPERS

Poor shopkeepers and craftsmen work hard to make a living. Some are slaves who have bought their freedom. They live in crowded blocks of flats in the city.

The rich people have pleasant, easy lives with lots of slaves to do all the work.

Livia married Petronius when she was only 12 years old. Her father chose her husband for her and gave Petronius' family a large sum of money, called a dowry. Livia looks after the house and has many slaves.

Claudia, the second daughter, is 12 and lives at home too. She has finished her schooling and now her mother is teaching her to spin and weave. A tutor gives her music and singing lessons.

CLAUDIA

AUNT ANTONIA

Petronius' sister, Antonia, and her two children, live with the family. Her husband was killed while fighting with the army. Now her brother gives her a home and looks after her.

RICH FRIENDS

Rich and important friends of Petronius are invited to his dinner parties. Some are army officers and government officials.

SLAVES

The poor people work hard to earn enough to eat. But the rich people give them cheap bread.

MARCUS

Marcus, Petronius' eldest son, is 16 years old. He is training to be a soldier in the Roman army. Like all children, even grown-up ones, he has to obey his father and ask his permission before he does anything.

Marius, the second son, is 15, and is learning about his father's business. When he is older, he will serve in the army for a while, like Marcus.

MARIUS

Sestius, Petronius' cousin, lives in a city far from Rome. He is visiting the family to ask for Petronius' help with some legal business.

SESTIUS   BUSINESSMEN

Business men come to Petronius for his advice, to beg for favours and to borrow money. Some also come to do favours for him.

The slaves in Petronius' house are captured foreigners who were bought at the slave market. If they run away, they may be beaten or put to death. But Petronius and Livia are kind to them. They are allowed to marry and have children. If they work hard, they may save up enough to buy their freedom.

On the Road to Rome

With the help of your Time Helmet, you have rushed back through nearly 2,000 years. It is A.D. 100. You are in Italy and on the road to Rome—the city away at the top of the picture.

Rome is now the biggest and most splendid city in the world. About 700 years before this time, it was a small village of wooden huts on one of the seven hills. Slowly the city has grown and fine stone houses, temples and public buildings have been built on all the hills.

As the city has grown bigger and richer, more people have come to live here. They have left their homes in the country and have learned to do all sorts of work.

The Romans have built good roads from their city so that their huge armies can march quickly along them. Look round you and see the people who travel to Rome. Turn over the page and you will be in the city itself.

Hunters have been shooting wild boar in the woods. Now they have stopped to cook meat over a fire.

At this tavern, travellers can buy food and drink and get a bed for the night. But they have to watch out for thieves who try to rob them.

TOMBSTONES

WINE JARS

A horseman carries official letters from the army commander in Britain to the emperor in Rome.

Milestones along the road mark out the distance to the middle of Rome in Roman miles.

ROAD MENDERS

This is Sestius who is going to stay with his cousin Petronius. Letters can take months to cross the empire so he visits Rome himself to settle a legal matter.

The paved roads are for fast traffic and important people. The slow farmcarts and poor people use the muddy tracks on each side.

Tombstones along the road mark the graves of people from Rome. No one is allowed to be buried inside the city boundaries.

4

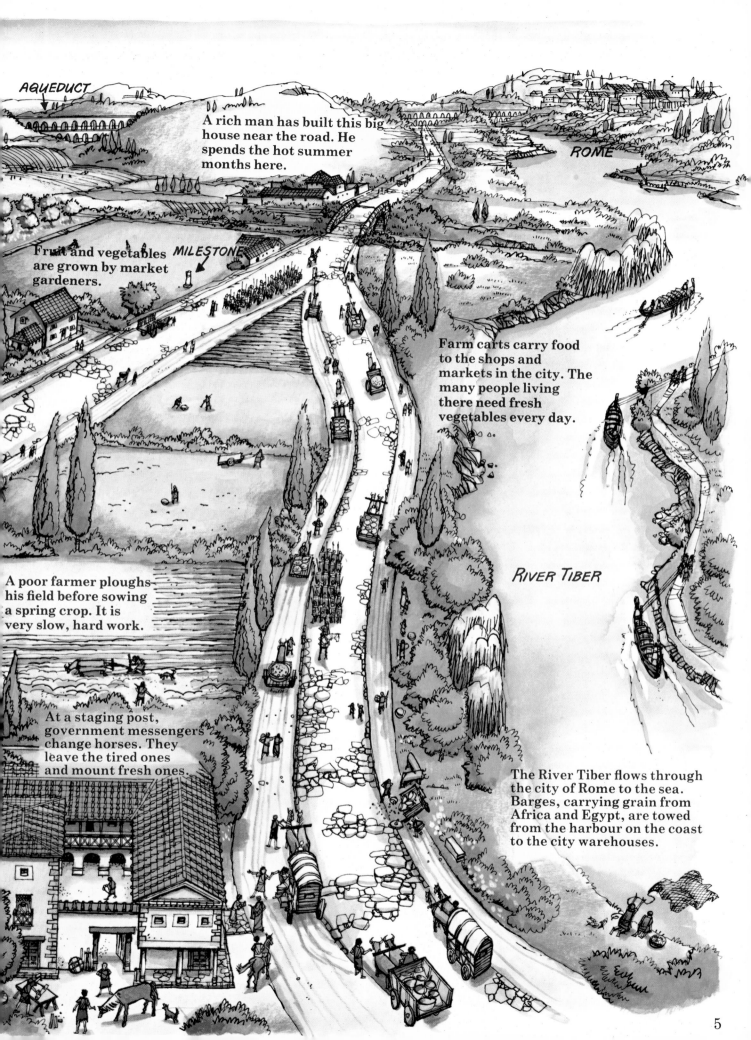

AQUEDUCT

A rich man has built this big house near the road. He spends the hot summer months here.

ROME

Fruit and vegetables are grown by market gardeners.

MILESTONE

Farm carts carry food to the shops and markets in the city. The many people living there need fresh vegetables every day.

A poor farmer ploughs his field before sowing a spring crop. It is very slow, hard work.

RIVER TIBER

At a staging post, government messengers change horses. They leave the tired ones and mount fresh ones.

The River Tiber flows through the city of Rome to the sea. Barges, carrying grain from Africa and Egypt, are towed from the harbour on the coast to the city warehouses.

5

In the Streets of Rome

The city of Rome is a marvellous place, with huge palaces, fine houses, baths, temples, arches, and theatres. They are built of stone and brick, held together with iron clamps and cement.

The important buildings were paid for by the emperors and the rich people. Many are covered with thin slabs of marble so they shine in the sun.

In the middle of Rome are open squares, called forums. They were built at different times and called after the emperors. The oldest and most important is the Roman Forum, thought to be the centre of the empire.

This huge sports arena, called the Colosseum, was built where a lake used to be. Now drains carry the water underground to the river.

AQUEDUCT

The poor people live in small houses and in flats. There have been so many big fires in Rome, they are not allowed to have cooking stoves upstairs.

The Forum of Peace was built by the emperor Vespasian. It is a quiet square with a library where people can read in peace.

Roman men come to this big ha called Basilica Aemilia, to do business, such as money chang

Firemen pump water through leather hoses to put out a fire.

In the Senate House, the most important men of Rome meet discuss government business. Foreign ambassadors are allo on to the platform in front of t Senate to hear the debates.

In Julius Caesar's market, small shops and stalls sell pepper, spices and all kinds of food.

PUBLIC LAVATORY

A dead man is carried in a litter, followed by his mourning family.

The empire is now so strong and safe, the city does not need walls to protect it from enemies. New houses and flats have been built far outside the old city walls.

The glittering white and gold palace has been made larger and more magnificent by the emperors. No ordinary people are allowed inside the garden walls.

This arch was put up by Augustus, the first emperor of Rome and the nephew of Julius Caesar. Lots of emperors had arches like this one built to celebrate their victories.

In the round temple, called the Temple of the Vestals, a fire burns all the time. It is looked after by young priestesses.

AMBASSADORS

TEMPLE OF CAESAR

SACRED WAY

THIEF

A procession of family and friends leads a bride to the house of the bridegroom on her wedding day.

Priests and officials lead animals to be sacrificed. When they have cut an animal open, an expert will look at its insides. From them, the Romans believe, he can tell if the gods favour them in battle.

This platform, called the New Rostra, is used by public speakers when talking to the people in the Forum.

Petronius at Home

This is where Petronius lives with his family, his sister, and his slaves and servants. Petronius is rich and an important man in Rome. His house is large and comfortable, although you would think it is rather bare of furniture and cold in the winter. There are stone floors and open roofs.

Like all Roman fathers, Petronius is the master of his household. Everyone has to obey him. But he is kind and treats his slaves and servants well. When he wants a new slave, he buys one at the market. The slaves are captured foreigners and may have a high price if they are young, healthy and skilful.

The Romans get up very early in the morning, usually before it is light, even in summer. Petronius does not go out to work but stays at home. Men come to see him to discuss their problems, borrow money or ask a favour. Important business men come to give favours and advice.

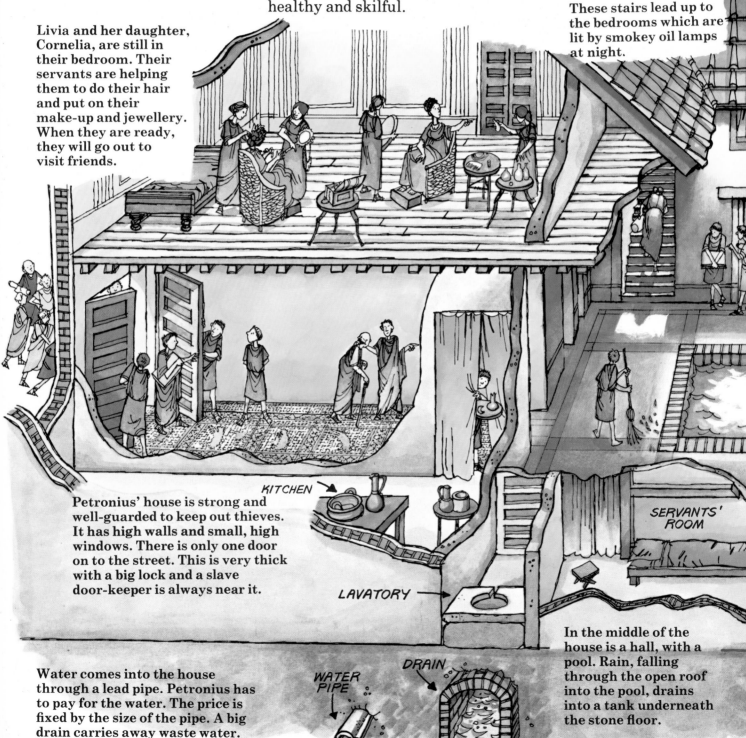

Livia and her daughter, Cornelia, are still in their bedroom. Their servants are helping them to do their hair and put on their make-up and jewellery. When they are ready, they will go out to visit friends.

These stairs lead up to the bedrooms which are lit by smokey oil lamps at night.

Petronius' house is strong and well-guarded to keep out thieves. It has high walls and small, high windows. There is only one door on to the street. This is very thick with a big lock and a slave door-keeper is always near it.

KITCHEN

SERVANTS' ROOM

LAVATORY

In the middle of the house is a hall, with a pool. Rain, falling through the open roof into the pool, drains into a tank underneath the stone floor.

Water comes into the house through a lead pipe. Petronius has to pay for the water. The price is fixed by the size of the pipe. A big drain carries away waste water.

DRAIN

WATER PIPE

Poor visitors have to wait for a long time in the hall or stand in a queue outside the front door. Important visitors are seen at once. When everyone has gone, Petronius will go out to see his friends or deal with a legal matter. He will also spend some time at the law courts.

Before Petronius sees the visitors, he puts on his toga. A slave carefully arranges the folds of the heavy woollen material. Only free citizens of Rome are allowed to wear togas. Petronius puts his on only for formal and state occasions.

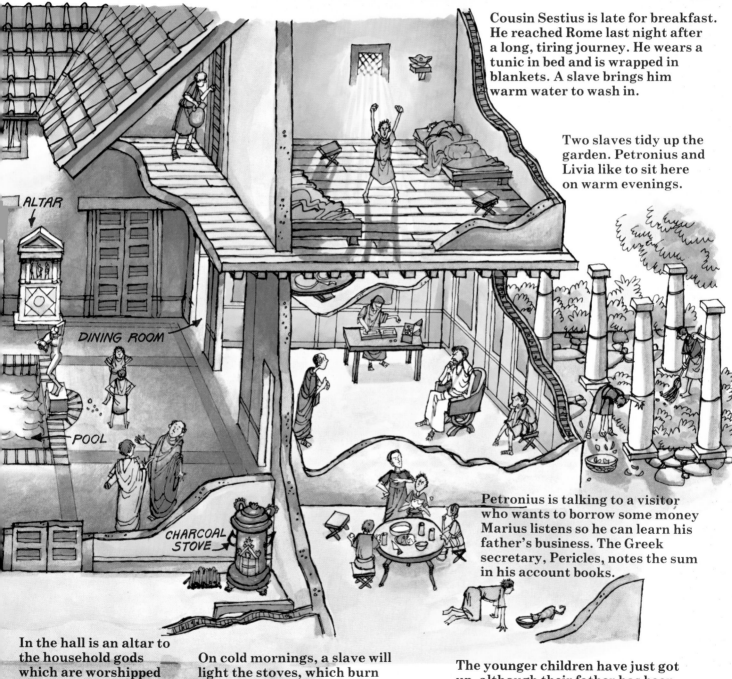

Cousin Sestius is late for breakfast. He reached Rome last night after a long, tiring journey. He wears a tunic in bed and is wrapped in blankets. A slave brings him warm water to wash in.

Two slaves tidy up the garden. Petronius and Livia like to sit here on warm evenings.

ALTAR

DINING ROOM

POOL

CHARCOAL STOVE

Petronius is talking to a visitor who wants to borrow some money. Marius listens so he can learn his father's business. The Greek secretary, Pericles, notes the sum in his account books.

In the hall is an altar to the household gods which are worshipped by the family.

On cold mornings, a slave will light the stoves, which burn charcoal—a special form of wood. There are no fireplaces or chimneys in the house, except for the cooking stoves in the kitchen.

The younger children have just got up, although their father has been at work for some time. They are eating a breakfast of bread, cheese and water, watched by Aunt Antonia.

Going to School

These boys are at a secondary school. They can go here after four or five years at primary school. They learn Greek and Latin grammar, arithmetic, geometry, history and all about the stars.

The boys are taught to speak and discuss in public. The Romans think this is very important.

Roman children go to school when they are about six or seven years old. Their fathers have to pay the schoolmasters. Some rich children are taught at home by private tutors who are often Greek slaves. Freed slaves start their own schools.

The schoolmasters are very strict and beat the children if they do not learn their lessons or are late. The schools start early in the morning when it is still dark. They end early in the afternoon so there is time for games or to go to the baths.

A BAKER GETS UP EARLY TO SELL NEW BUNS TO SCHOOL CHILDREN.

A BOY LIGHTS HIS WAY TO SCHOOL WITH A TORCH.

OIL LAMP

FAMOUS WRITER

THIS BOY FORGOT HIS LESSON.

SCHOOL FOR OLDER BOYS.

A slave takes a boy to school and carries his bag with wax tablets and pens.

Games

Roman children play lots of games in the streets when lessons are over. There are no school games or playgrounds for them.

Hoops are fun for rolling and jumping through.

Fights with wooden swords can be quite fierce.

BALLS ARE MADE OF LEATHER.

Two girls play a game called jacks with five small bones and a ball.

Stick and ball games have no proper rules so you can make them up as you play.

Wax Tablets

Schoolchildren write on boards spread with wax. They scratch words or sums in the wax with the point of a stick. They can rub out with the flat end of the stick.

Scrolls

Roman books are rolls of paper, called scrolls, and are written by hand. Each end of the roll is stuck to a rod. You have to unroll the paper to read each page.

Pens and Ink

People write on the scrolls with pens made of small reeds or of copper. The ink in the pot is a sticky mixture of soot, pitch and the black ink from an octopus.

FAMOUS THINKER

SCHOOL MASTER

WHEN IT IS DARK IN THE MORNING NO ONE SEES A BOY DRAWING ON A WALL.

THIS BOY IS RECITING A LESSON HE HAS LEARNED.

A GIRL WRITES ON A WAX TABLET.

Most schools are in the porches of buildings. A curtain stops people in the street from looking into the classroom.

At this primary school, boys and girls learn to read and write and do simple arithmetic. There are no books or paper to write on.

Every eighth day is a holiday. Then markets are set up in the streets and it is much too noisy to have lessons at school.

JAVELINS

Boys and girls learn to swim by holding on to bamboo floats.

Boys racing their carts pretend they are real charioteers.

Shops and Markets

The shops of Rome are small and dark. They are kept by the poor people and by freed slaves. In some streets are the workshops of craftsmen, such as weavers, silversmiths and shoe-makers.

Rich people go shopping only for clothes, jewels and other expensive things. They send their servants or slaves to buy food and wine and to take their clothes to the cleaners.

Meat, fruit and vegetables are brought from the gardens and farms outside the city. Noisy wooden carts carry everything to the shops and markets very early in the morning.

At the bakery, wheat is ground into flour. It is mixed into dough and baked in the oven.

WHEAT

OVEN

STONE MILL

FLOUR

DOUGH

PIG FED ON SCRAPS

The new loaves are sold at the bakery. There is no paper to wrap them in. The loaves have dents in them to make them easier to cut.

People meet in the noisy, dusty, and often smelly streets. They stop to gossip and hear the latest news of the wars and the empire.

Livia and Petronius are shown woollen and cotton material by the cloth merchants. Livia wants a new tunic to wear at a feast.

At the chemist's, a man has an ointment made of herbs, flowers and seeds put in his eyes. Ill people also buy magic spells.

Rich Romans send their clothes to special shops to be cleaned. Men, called fullers, spread them on frames to bleach them.

Then the fullers put them in tubs of water and a special clay. They tread on the clothes to get the dirt out.

The clothes are dried and folded and then put in a big press to flatten them. There are no irons in Rome.

A slave collects the clean clothes for his master. He makes sure the work has been done well before he pays.

The Market

Today is a market day. Stalls, with awnings to keep off the hot sun, are set up in a city square. They sell fruit and vegetables, meat and fish. Musicians play to earn a few coins from the crowd.

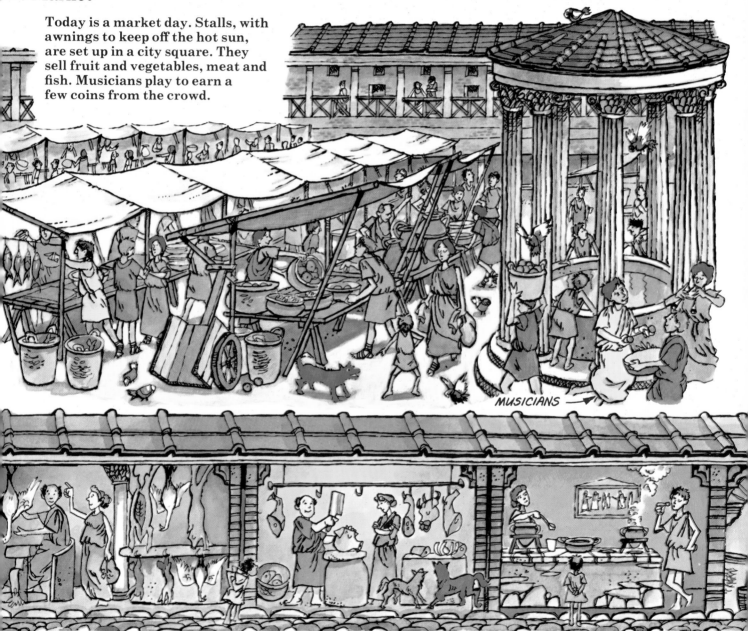

MUSICIANS →

A customer chooses a goose to be cooked for a special feast. Usually only the men slaves and servants do the household shopping.

A butcher chops up a pig's head in his shop. Only rich people can afford to eat meat every day. The poor fill up with cheap food.

This shop sells hot food for people to eat in the streets or take home with them. Many flats and houses have no cooking stoves.

13

Afternoon at the Baths

Petronius goes to the baths in the afternoons when his work is done. The baths are not only for washing but are good places to meet friends, have business meetings and hear the latest gossip. Some men go there to do exercises, walk in the gardens or read in a quiet room.

Livia and her friends go to the women's baths or to these baths in the morning when men are not allowed in.

There are lots of baths in Rome. They cost very little and some are free. Only very rich people have baths in their houses.

Everyone leaves their clothes and sandals on the shelves in the changing room.

Some men live in the flats built round the cold bath. It is very noisy because the bathers sing, whistle, shout and argue.

This is the cold bath for cooling down after the warm bath and for swimming.

Hungry bathers can buy honey cakes from the pastry cook.

WRESTLERS

People can walk and talk privately in the cool gardens.

Dirty water goes into a huge tunnel under the baths. This drain has been dug under Rome and empties into the river.

14

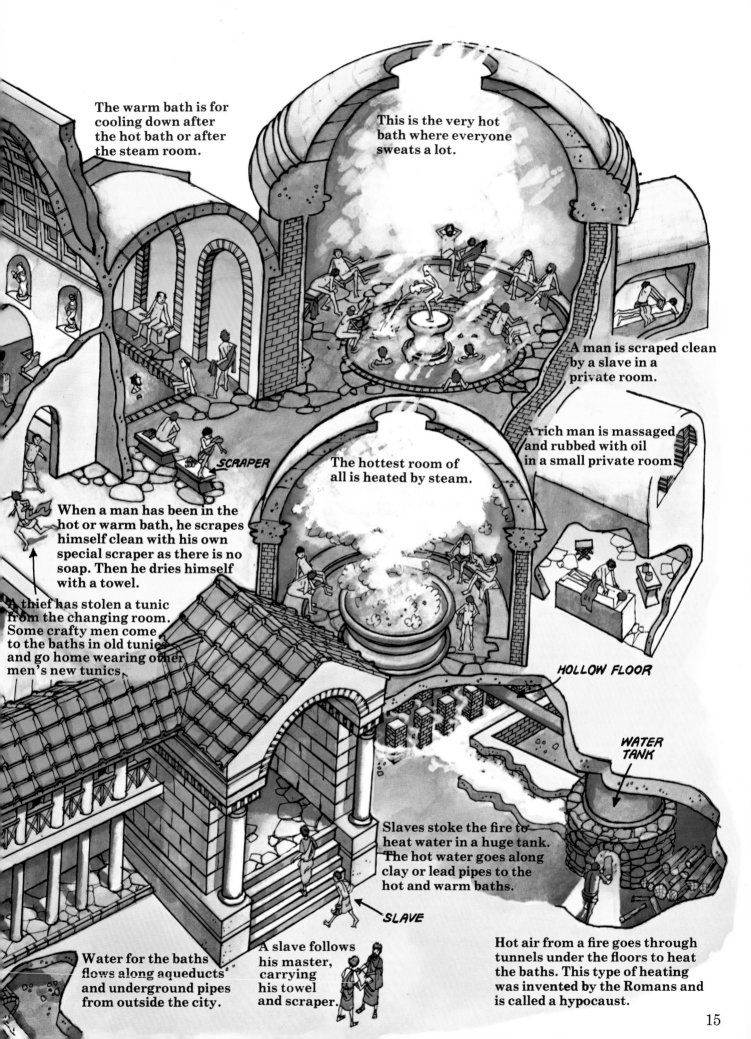

The warm bath is for cooling down after the hot bath or after the steam room.

This is the very hot bath where everyone sweats a lot.

A man is scraped clean by a slave in a private room.

A rich man is massaged and rubbed with oil in a small private room.

The hottest room of all is heated by steam.

SCRAPER

When a man has been in the hot or warm bath, he scrapes himself clean with his own special scraper as there is no soap. Then he dries himself with a towel.

A thief has stolen a tunic from the changing room. Some crafty men come to the baths in old tunics and go home wearing other men's new tunics.

HOLLOW FLOOR

WATER TANK

Slaves stoke the fire to heat water in a huge tank. The hot water goes along clay or lead pipes to the hot and warm baths.

SLAVE

Water for the baths flows along aqueducts and underground pipes from outside the city.

A slave follows his master, carrying his towel and scraper.

Hot air from a fire goes through tunnels under the floors to heat the baths. This type of heating was invented by the Romans and is called a hypocaust.

15

Gladiators and Charioteers

Gladiator fights and chariot races are the favourite sports of the Romans. At festivals and public holidays, people flock to the arenas and race tracks.

In the arena, prisoners and criminals are put to death. Some are attacked by hungry wild animals. Some are made to fight each other or are killed by the fierce gladiators.

At the race track, the emperor, rich men, noble ladies, poor people and children shout with excitement as the little carts speed round the course.

The biggest sports stadium in Rome is called the Colosseum. It can seat 45,000 people. A huge awning shades them from the sun.

Each of the 76 public entrances has a number. They are written on the tickets so people can easily find their way to their seats.

Gladiators are men who have been condemned to death. They are trained at special schools to fight and die very bravely.

Thousands of wild animals are brought to Rome for the fights. They are captured in parts of the empire as far away as North Africa.

Gladiators have different kinds of weapons to make the fights more exciting. The net fighter tries to dodge a sharp sword.

When he gets a chance, he flings his net over his enemy. He tries to tangle him up in it and stab with his fisherman's spear.

The wounded man begs for mercy. If the crowd gives the 'thumbs up' sign, he will live. 'Thumbs down' means he must die.

1

At the start of a race, the chariots wait at the starting line. Each charioteer leans forward, balancing the light, wood and leather cart with his weight.

2

The trumpet sounds, the starter drops his white flag, and they are off. Leaning back against the reins, the drivers beat their horses with stinging whips.

3

If the carts crash, or a wheel comes off, or a horse stumbles, the driver pulls out his dagger. Quickly he cuts the reins to stop him being dragged by the horses.

The Circus

Chariot races are held at the huge track called the Circus. Before the races start, priests and officials walk in procession round the track.

The horses race round the track seven times. The winning driver is given a purse full of gold and treated like a hero.

People bet on the drivers, choosing him by the colour of his tunic. They wave coloured banners and cheer to encourage him.

The turning posts at the ends of the track are the most dangerous places for the chariots and horses.

Only the best and luckiest drivers come out alive from a crash, called a 'shipwreck' by the Romans.

The charioteers wear metal helmets to protect their heads, and pads and leather bandages on their legs.

17

Building in the City

The city of Rome is always noisy with the sound of building. Old houses are pulled down. Sometimes they burn down or just fall down. New and bigger ones are built in their places.

New houses and blocks of flats are built by the poor people. Palaces, temples, bridges over the river, arches and aqueducts are paid for by rich people and by the emperor.

These men are building a new aqueduct. When it is finished, it will carry fresh water to fountains in the city where people get their water, and to the baths.

Stone for building is brought in big wooden carts from the quarries outside the city.

STONE BLOCKS

RUBBISH

Broken stone and building rubble is taken away to the rubbish dumps.

The rich people like the walls of their houses painted with pictures. These are called murals. An artist paints on wet plaster while her assistant mixes the colours.

This man is building a wall of bricks made of baked clay. He lays them down carefully and sticks them together with mortar. This is a mixture of sand, mud and water.

MURAL

ASSISTANT

PIECES OF MARBLE

PLASTER   TILES

This man spreads plaster over the new brick wall.

These men are laying the floor. It is made of coloured marble, set out in a pattern.

Carving a Tombstone

The carpenters make wooden shapes to hold up the arches while the stones are put in place. The scaffolding is taken away when the arch is complete.

A crane lifts heavy stones up to the top of the columns.

A mason is carving a tomb stone for a rich man. Even poor people save up to buy tomb stones for themselves.

The stone is carved to show portraits of the man and his son. The pictures of tools show the man made coins.

Now the mason carefully cuts letters into the stone. You can read the man's name: P. Licinius Philonicus.

WOODEN SHAPE FOR ARCH

CRANE

SCAFFOLDING

Tree trunks are sawn into planks by carpenters. They make the frames, doors and windows for houses.

CRANE

CARPENTERS

The stone workers, called masons, are always busy. They carve the pillars and big stones for temples, arches and other public buildings.

STONE MASONS

New tiles are put on the roof of a house. They overlap each other so that no water gets through.

CARPENTERS

How to Make a Mosaic

MOSAIC FLOOR. WET PLASTER.

BITS OF GLASS AND STONE.

WET PLASTER

The craftsman spreads wet plaster over a small patch of the floor and smooths it down.

Then he presses little squares of glass or stone into the plaster. Bit by bit, he makes up a coloured picture.

When the picture is finished, he rubs more plaster over it to fill in the small gaps between the squares.

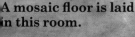

A mosaic floor is laid in this room.

19

Petronius Gives a Feast

The Romans spend their evenings at home. The rich give feasts for their friends and important people of the city. Poor people, who cannot afford oil for lamps, usually go to bed when it gets dark.

Tonight Petronius has asked some friends to dinner. All day, his servants and slaves have been hard at work preparing the food. You would think some of it is strange and tastes very nasty.

The poor people have cheap, dull food. Meat and fish are often too expensive for them to buy so they eat wheat cooked to make a sort of porridge. Sometimes a rich man will give a feast for them.

Slaves have carried this lady to the feast in a litter.

This guest is late but no one minds. There are no clocks, only sun dials and hour glasses in Rome, so it is hard to be on time.

Meat is roasted over an open fire. Sauces and vegetables are cooked in pots on a stove.

Everyone in the kitchen is very busy. It is hot and dark, and dirty with the smoke from lamps.

These two slaves brought their master to Petronius' house. They play dice while waiting until the feast is over. A slave brings them some supper.

Cooking

FISH
WINE
HERBS
HONEY   PEPPER

The head cook is making a special sauce for a meat dish. He pounds up the insides of fish with herbs, spices, wine and honey.

MARROWS   BEANS   ONIONS.   PEAS   LETTUCE

Two slaves chop up beans, onions, asparagus, lettuce and garlic. The vegetables will be eaten raw for the first course.

OYSTERS   SNAILS

Live snails left in milk for two days have grown fat. One slave takes them out of their shells while another opens oysters.

Less important guests eat at this table. The food is not so costly and does not look so nice.

Musicians play a pipe and a string instrument, called a cithera, to entertain the guests as they talk.

A man who has been to Britain tells the story of his slow, difficult journey. It took many months with lots of adventures.

This is the chief guest. He is so busy, he dictates letters to his secretary while he eats his dinner.

A poet waits to recite some of his own poems.

This table is for the family and the most important guests. They have the very costly and nicest food.

Guests wash their hands between courses. They may slip food into their napkins to take home with them.

Everyone eats with their fingers from the big dishes carried round by the slaves. They can choose to eat the things they like best.

When they are full, the people drink and talk. They discuss such things as whether the chicken or egg came first; why men can see to read better when they are old; if wrestling is the oldest sport.

First Course

← OIL AND EGG SAUCE

STUFFED DORMICE

PEACOCKS' EGGS

The first course is a dish of stuffed and cooked dormice, stuffed olives and prunes, and peacocks' eggs with a sauce.

Main Course

CHICKEN

DEER

OSTRICH

DOVES

LOBSTER

BABY PIG

BOAR'S HEAD

All sorts of boiled and roast meat is served for the second course. The meat is sliced by the slaves as the guests do not have any knives or forks.

Third Course

FRUIT

HONEY CAKES

STUFFED DATES

The last course is a big glass bowl of fruit, a plate of dates and little cakes sweetened with honey. After this, the guests drink wine to each other's health.

Summer in the Country

During the summer, Rome is very hot and uncomfortable. Many people die of fever. Petronius takes his family and personal servants to his estate outside the city. He likes to spend some time in the country.

The estate has a big house, called a villa, in the middle of the farmland. There are rooms for the farm workers. The part where the family live is more grand and comfortable.

September is a busy time on the farm. The wheat, which ripens early in the hot Italian sun, has already been cut. Now the grapes and olives are picked to make wine and oil. All the food has to be stored for the winter.

At the end of the month, Petronius will take his family back to the house in Rome.

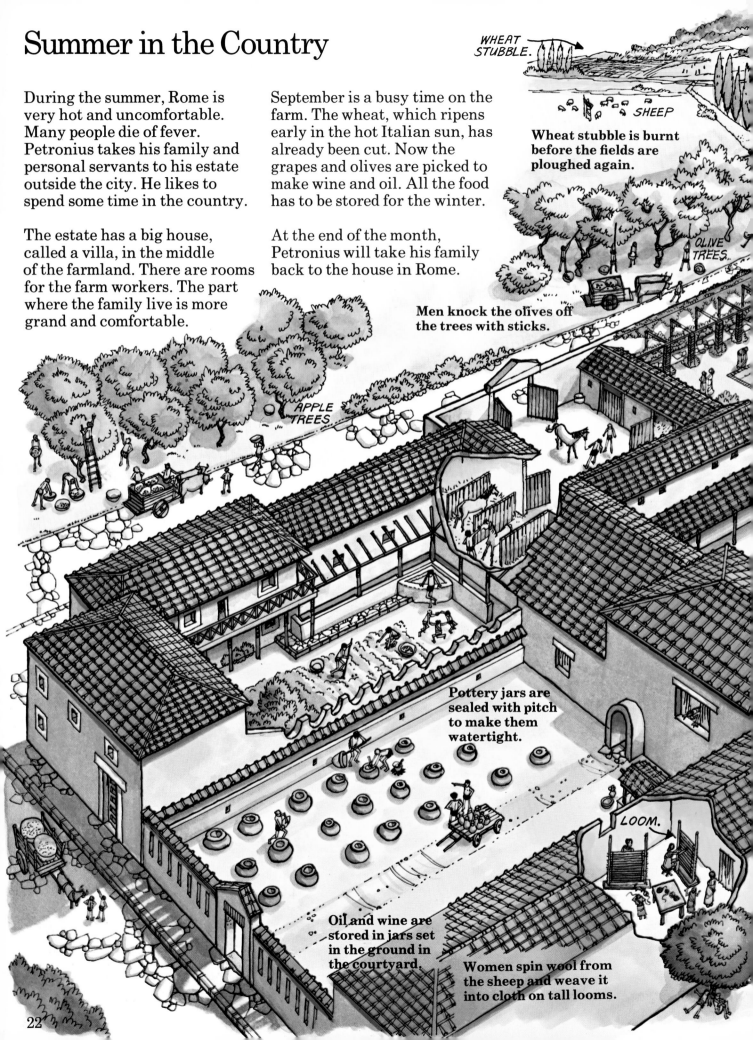

WHEAT STUBBLE.

SHEEP

Wheat stubble is burnt before the fields are ploughed again.

OLIVE TREES.

Men knock the olives off the trees with sticks.

APPLE TREES

Pottery jars are sealed with pitch to make them watertight.

LOOM.

Oil and wine are stored in jars set in the ground in the courtyard.

Women spin wool from the sheep and weave it into cloth on tall looms.

22

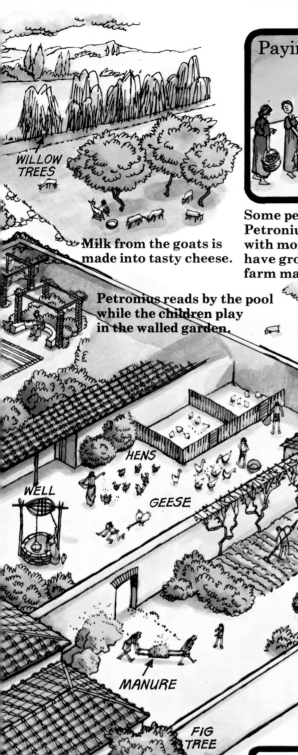

WILLOW TREES

Milk from the goats is made into tasty cheese.

Petronius reads by the pool while the children play in the walled garden.

WELL

HENS

GEESE

PIGS

MANURE

FIG TREE

A slave weaves baskets of sticks cut from the willows by the stream.

Paying the Rent

Some peasants lease land from Petronius. They pay rent for it with money, with the food they have grown, or with animals. The farm manager writes it all down.

Pressing Olives

When the ripe olives have been harvested, they are put into a screw press. Workers wind the handles to squash the olives and squeeze out the precious oil.

The bunches of ripe grapes are picked off the vines and put into baskets. Then they are taken to the villa for making into wine.

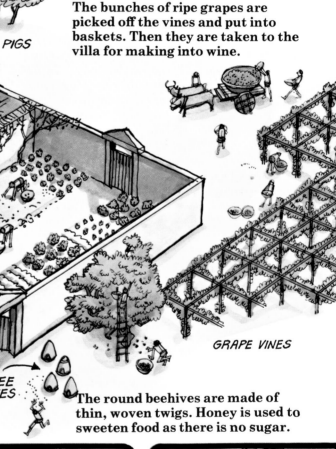

GRAPE VINES

BEE HIVES

The round beehives are made of thin, woven twigs. Honey is used to sweeten food as there is no sugar.

1 Making Wine

The grapes are tipped into a big stone trough. The men tread on them to squash out the juice. They have sticks to stop them slipping over on the mushy grape skins.

2

The grape skins are then put into a press to squeeze out the rest of the juice. The juice is put into big jars. It bubbles and foams as it turns into wine.

Marcus Joins the Army

Petronius' son, Marcus, is now 16 and is joining the Roman army. He has been sent to a camp, with other new recruits, many days' journey from Rome. Here he will be taught all the things soldiers have to do when they are fighting the enemy.

Thousands of soldiers live in the camps, guarding the frontiers of the Roman empire. The camps are surrounded by strong stone walls and some are so big, they are like towns. Cities often grow up round them as people move near to sell food and clothes to the troops.

At the camp, Marcus and other new soldiers have their names written down in the army record book. He swears an oath and promises to be loyal to the emperor. He will swear this oath again every year.

First Marcus is measured by an army tailor who will make his uniform. He will wear a tunic and armour made of metal and leather.

Next he tries on bronze helmets for size. They are lined with leather to protect his head.

Now the training begins. It will make the young recruits strong and good at fighting. They start with drill, marching twice a day, carrying spears and heavy packs.

Training

Marcus learns to fight by running at a target with a wooden sword. He and the other boys fight mock battles with swords and spears.

Horse riding is more fun but everyone laughs when Marcus falls off. There are no stirrups for his feet so he has to balance in the saddle wearing heavy armour.

The recruits learn to lock their shields together to make a 'tortoise'. This will protect them from enemy arrows and stones. But it is not easy for beginners.

The Fortress

When the soldiers came here many years ago, they built a strong stone camp. People now live near the camp and have put up shops and houses round the walls.

Part of the army has gone out on a long expedition. The soldiers left to guard the camp have time to repair the walls and grow vegetables in their gardens.

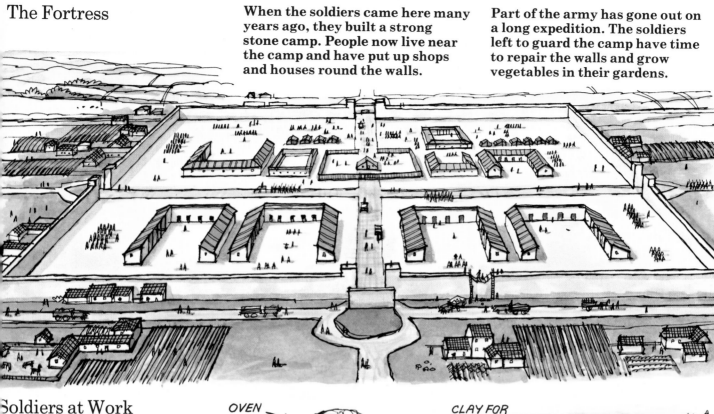

Soldiers at Work

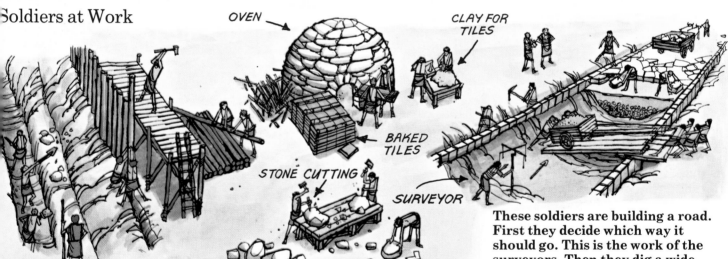

OVEN

CLAY FOR TILES

BAKED TILES

STONE CUTTING

SURVEYOR

The recruits learn to dig ditches and set up wooden walls. When marching through enemy territory, they will make a camp of turf and wooden stakes every night.

Soldiers have to learn all sorts of things, like cutting and shaping stones, and making roof tiles.

These soldiers are building a road. First they decide which way it should go. This is the work of the surveyors. Then they dig a wide ditch and fill it with broken stone. On top go big flat stones. The road slopes down each side so that rain water runs off quickly.

1 Firing a Catapult

2

3

Today Marcus is taught how to fire a catapult. The officer watches as the soldiers wind down the huge beam with its sling.

Then a loader lifts a large stone into the sling. This can weigh as much as 30 kilos.

When they fire the catapult, the stone is flung into the air and lands about 30 metres away. It can easily smash holes in enemy walls.

Attacking a Citadel

Marcus has finished his training and is now a junior officer. He has been sent out with a large army from the main camp.

After many weeks' march, they crossed the River Danube into Romania in Eastern Europe. The Dacians, who live here, have been massing their forces and threatening Roman lands.

When the Romans reached a small Dacian settlement, they attacked it and took many prisoners. Now the Dacians have retreated to their hill-top citadel to fight off the Roman siege. This is Marcus' first real battle and he hopes to prove his skill and courage.

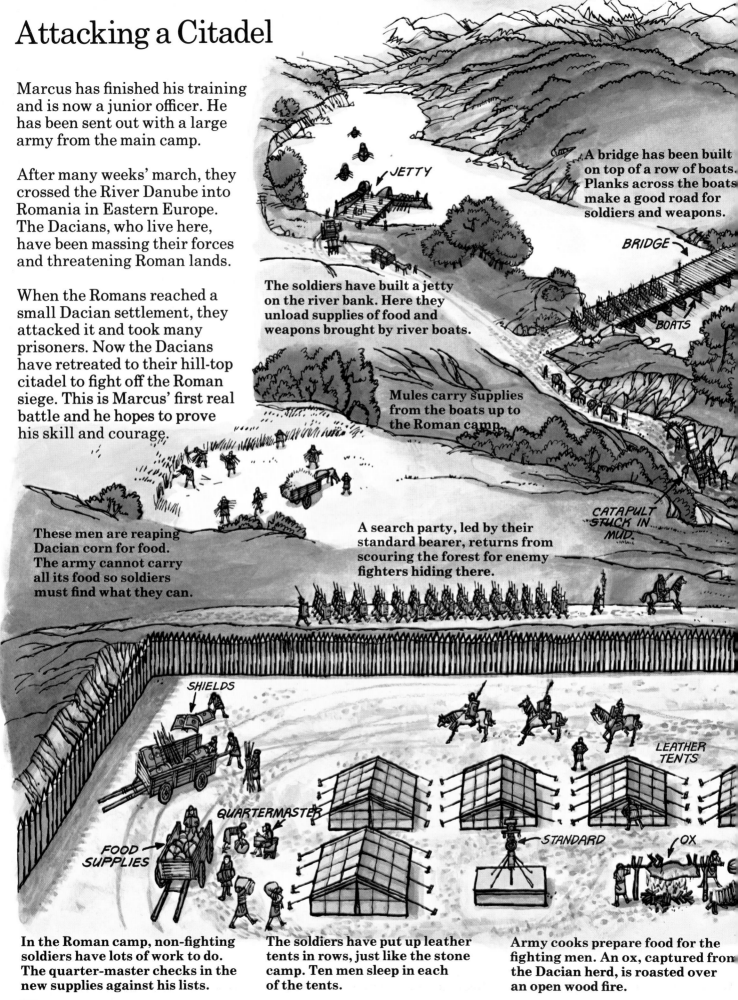

JETTY

A bridge has been built on top of a row of boats. Planks across the boats make a good road for soldiers and weapons.

BRIDGE

BOATS

The soldiers have built a jetty on the river bank. Here they unload supplies of food and weapons brought by river boats.

Mules carry supplies from the boats up to the Roman camp.

CATAPULT STUCK IN MUD.

These men are reaping Dacian corn for food. The army cannot carry all its food so soldiers must find what they can.

A search party, led by their standard bearer, returns from scouring the forest for enemy fighters hiding there.

SHIELDS

LEATHER TENTS

QUARTERMASTER

STANDARD

OX

FOOD SUPPLIES

In the Roman camp, non-fighting soldiers have lots of work to do. The quarter-master checks in the new supplies against his lists.

The soldiers have put up leather tents in rows, just like the stone camp. Ten men sleep in each of the tents.

Army cooks prepare food for the fighting men. An ox, captured from the Dacian herd, is roasted over an open wood fire.

26

Roman soldiers burn down the thatched huts in the Dacian village.

Catapults fling stones at the fighters in the Dacian citadel. Flaming missiles set fire to the wooden walls and defence towers.

Under a 'tortoise' of shields, soldiers march safely up to the citadel.

CATAPULTS

These Moorish horsemen, rounding up Dacian cattle, are from North Africa. They are fierce, wild men who fight with the Roman army.

COMMANDER

The Roman commander watches the attack. From here he can direct his troops. Marcus brings him a message from another officer and will carry back his orders.

MARCUS

REINFORCEMENTS

PRISONERS

BAKE OVENS

GRINDING WHEAT

WOUNDED SOLDIERS

DACIAN PRISONERS

The bakers grind wheat into flour and mix it into dough. It is cooked to make hard, dry biscuits.

Wounded soldiers are looked after by army doctors. There is no hospital at the temporary camp.

Dacian prisoners are kept in a stockade. They will be sold as slaves when the battle is over.

The Roman Empire

Now move the flight stick on your Time Travelling Helmet and hover far above Rome. From a great height, you can look down on the map of the empire spread out below you and see how big it was a few years after your trip. It then took in most of Europe and surrounded the Mediterranean.

The capital city of Rome and other big cities in the empire were built near the sea and on rivers. This was so the food and all the other things needed by people living there could be brought by ships and barges. Look round the map and see where everything comes from and how it gets to Rome.

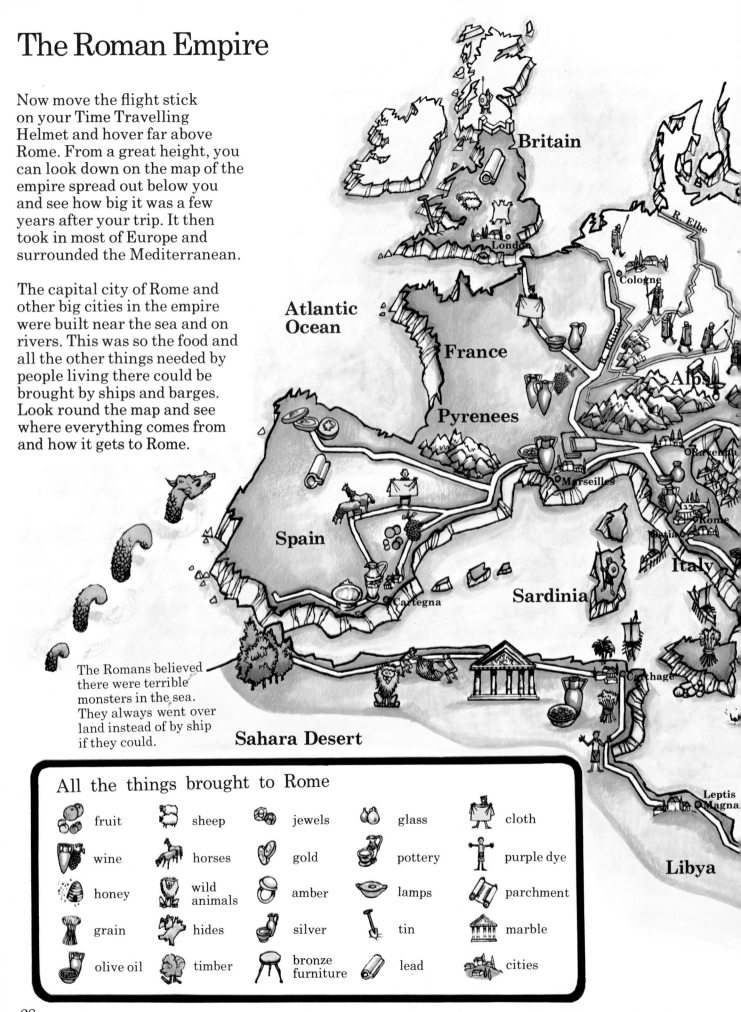

Britain

London

Atlantic Ocean

R. Elbe

Cologne

France

Pyrenees

Alps

Marseilles

Ravenna

Rome

Ostia

Spain

Italy

Cartegna

Sardinia

The Romans believed there were terrible monsters in the sea. They always went over land instead of by ship if they could.

Sahara Desert

Carthage

Leptis Magna

Libya

All the things brought to Rome

fruit	sheep	jewels	glass	cloth
wine	horses	gold	pottery	purple dye
honey	wild animals	amber	lamps	parchment
grain	hides	silver	tin	marble
olive oil	timber	bronze furniture	lead	cities

The Romans called the people who lived outside their empire 'barbarians', which means foreigners. Some of these people did not live in cities, like the Romans, but travelled about. They moved in search of new land they could farm to grow crops of food and where they could graze their animals.

Sometimes they attacked the Roman frontiers to reach the land inside the empire. In the second century A.D., some of these barbarians fought their way right into Italy.

In the fourth century A.D., thousands of barbarians invaded Roman territories. They swept down from the north-east, destroying towns and cities, burning farms and killing the people. After they had captured Roman land, they settled down to farm it.

The Roman armies were driven back. The emperors could not get enough soldiers or money to fight the invasion, although the Roman people were taxed very heavily and were sometimes short of food.

The huge empire gradually grew smaller as the Roman armies lost their battles and were scattered. The barbarians even captured the city of Rome itself.

R. Vistula
Barbarians
Barbarians
R. Dniester
R. Dnieper
slaves
Romania (Dacia)
R. Danube
Caspian Sea
salt
Black Sea
camel train
silk from China
Greece
Constantinople
shipbuilding
Syria
Athens
Dura-Europos
Desert
Antioch
paper and jewels from the East
Cyprus
Palmyra
Crete
Lebanon
Sidon
Tyre
Damascus
Mediterranean Sea
grain ships
Judaea
Alexandria
Cairo
Petra
Egypt
R. Nile
Red Sea
Desert

Roman soldiers built thousands of miles of long, straight roads in the empire. They crossed mountains, rivers, marshes and deserts. The roads were so well made, some are still used today. All over Europe and North Africa are the remains of Roman towns, villas, forts, baths and walls. Some are just heaps of stone. But in some places you can really see where the Romans lived nearly 2,000 years ago.

29

The Story of Rome

The story of Rome began in about 753 B.C. when some wandering people from Northern Europe reached a hill near the River Tiber in Italy. They built a village and settled down to grow crops and keep cattle and sheep. Soon the village grew and huts were built on the other hills. Later the villages joined up into a city and a trading centre, ruled by kings.

The people got rid of their king, in 509 B.C., and set up a republic, choosing two consuls each year to rule instead. The Romans fought and conquered their neighbours to protect their land. Gradually they captured more and more territory until by 250 B.C., they controlled the whole of Italy.

The Roman armies were strong and brave but, when war broke out with the people of Carthage, in 260 B.C., they had to learn to fight at sea. They built a huge fleet of fighting ships and soon won great battles against these fierce sea-going people, whose main city was in North Africa. The Carthaginians built a new base in Spain so they could attack the Romans.

In Spain, a young army commander, called Hannibal, built up a huge army. Many of Rome's enemies joined him and they marched, with 36 elephants, over the Alps into Northern Italy. He won many battles but the Romans cut off Hannibal's supply lines and stopped him reaching Rome.

The Romans landed in North Africa, in 204 B.C., to attack the city of Carthage. Hannibal sailed home to defend it but Carthage was defeated. Later, the Romans besieged the city and, in 146 B.C., completely destroyed it. The people were killed or sold as slaves.

The defeat of Carthage made Rome the greatest power in the Mediterranean. At home, the rich people lived in great luxury with slaves to work in their houses and on their farms. But they were greedy and paid people to elect them as state officials. In the provinces, some governors made their subjects pay huge taxes and robbed them.

Civil war broke out in Rome when two generals tried to grab power. One marched his troops through the streets, killing everyone he did not like. Then in 73 B.C. Spartacus, a slave, led a revolt. He escaped to Mount Vesuvius and was joined by 90,000 slaves. He fought off the Roman army until he was killed in 71 B.C.

Two generals, Julius Caesar and Pompey, struggled for control of the government. Caesar marched from Gaul to Rome but Pompey left for Greece. Caesar defeated Pompey's army there but Pompey escaped to Egypt where he was murdered. Caesar went to Egypt and made Cleopatra queen. After more conquests he returned to Rome.

In 45 B.C. Caesar became sole ruler of Rome. He used his power to bring justice to the people and planned to improve the city. But he had many enemies who feared he would become king. In 44 B.C. he was stabbed to death in the Senate.

Caesar's nephew and heir, Octavian, defeated the last of Caesar's enemies when he won a great sea battle against Antony. Antony, and later his friend, Cleopatra killed themselves. Octavian then became head of the state and its first emperor.

Octavian took the name of Augustus. He built up the armies to guard the Roman frontiers against invaders. He tried to conquer land north of the River Rhine but lost a terrible battle against German tribes. In the empire, people settled down to build new cities. The government built roads to bring peace and trade.

When Augustus died in A.D. 14, members of his family succeeded him. But the emperor was not a king and anyone who had enough support could come to power. In one year, there were four emperors, each put forward by different groups of soldiers. Later in the first century A.D., men who had not even been born in Rome became emperors.

In A.D. 117, Hadrian was made emperor because he was a good general. He strengthened the frontiers and built a great stone wall across the north of Britain to keep out the barbarians. In Judaea, the Roman army put down a revolt by the Jews and thousands were killed.

Early in the second century A.D. the empire reached its greatest extent. But the barbarians were attacking the frontiers. Southern German tribes were pushed forward by the tribes behind them and they swept into northern Italy. They were defeated but still threatened Rome's northern and eastern borders of the empire.

In the third century A.D., Rome's armies became a strong influence on the affairs of government. Many emperors were created by the troops and ruled for very short periods. The vast empire was very hard to control and there were many civil wars. Old enemies, such as the Persians, took the chance to regain land they had lost and even kidnapped and killed the emperor Valerian.

People who lived in the empire became afraid of the barbarians and no longer believed Roman might could protect them. Soldiers posted across the empire spread new religions from the East and many people became Christians. When the emperors wanted to blame someone for the troubles in the empire, they blamed Christians and many were put to death.

For a few years, the empire was saved by the emperor Diocletian. But there was not enough money to pay the armies needed to fight off the invaders.

The next ruler, Constantine, won a battle to become emperor with the Christian sign on his standard. He made Christianity the state religion in A.D. 320 and set up a new capital in the east, called Constantinople, after him. The eastern, and stronger, half of the empire was ruled from there. It held back outside enemies until 1453 when it was overrun by the Turks. But the barbarians invaded the western half of the Roman empire and, in A.D. 410, they sacked Rome. A barbarian made himself ruler of Italy in 476 and the empire was destroyed.

After the barbarians overran the empire, many Roman things remained. The barbarians became Christians, and Latin—the Roman language—became the language of the Church. The languages now spoken in France, Spain, Italy and Portugal all developed from Latin and there are many Latin words in Dutch, German and English. Roman ideas of law and justice have been adopted by Western law and many cities have copied the Roman style.

Index

Altars 9
Aqueducts 6, 15, 18–19
Ambassadors 6
Army,
   camps 24–5, 26–7
   Dacian 26–7
   Roman 24–5, 26–7, 29, 30–1
   training 24–5
   uniform 24

Bakers, 10, 12
   army 27
Baths, 14–15
   water for 15, 18
Books 11, 23
Bread 10, 12
Building 18–19

Carts,
   farm 5, 6, 12
   racing 17
   toy 11
Catapults 25, 27
Chariot races 16, 17
Cheese 9, 23
Chemists 12
Circus, the 17
Clothes, 8–9, 12, 13
   cleaning 13
Colosseum 6, 16
Cooking, 4, 6, 13, 20
   army 26–7
Cooking stoves 6, 9, 13, 20

Dacians 26–7, 28–9
Drains 6, 8, 14

Emperors, 6–7, 24 ,30–1
   palace 7
Empire, Roman 6, 7, 28–9, 30–1

Farmers 5, 22–3
Feasts 20–1
Firemen 6
Flour 12, 27
Food 5, 6, 9, 12–13, 20–1, 22–3
Forums 6
Fruit 5, 6, 13, 21
Fullers 13

Games, 16–17
   children's 10–11
Gladiators 16
Grapes 21, 22, 23

Honey, 20, 21, 23
   cakes 14, 21
Horses 5, 17, 24
Houses 5, 6, 7, 8, 18–19, 22, 25
Hypocaust 15

Ink 11

Julius Caesar 7, 30

Lamps 8, 10, 11, 20, 21
Litters 6, 20
Looms 22

Markets 6, 11, 13
Masons 19
Meat 4, 13, 20, 21, 26
Mosaics 19
Musicians 13, 21

Pens 11

Olive oil 22, 23
Olives 21, 22, 23

Priests 7, 17

Races,
   chariot 17
   children's 11
Rivers,
   Danube 26
   Tiber 5
Roads 4, 25, 28–9
Rome,
   baths 14–15
   buildings 6–7, 18–19
   city of 4, 6–7
   shops 12–13
   sports 16–17
   story of 30–1
Senate House 7, 30
Schoolmasters 10–11
Schools 10–11
Scrolls 11
Shops 6, 11, 12–13
Slaves 8–9, 10, 20–1, 29
Soldiers 4, 5, 24–5, 26–7, 29, 30–1
Spices 6, 20
Staging posts 5
Swimming 11

Taverns 4
Temples 6, 7, 18
Tiber, River 5, 6–7
Togas 9
Tombstones 4, 19

Vegetables 5, 6, 13, 20, 25
Villas 5, 22

Water 4, 8, 14, 15, 18
Weaving 22
Wheat 12, 20, 22, 26, 27
Wine 20, 21, 22, 23
Writing 11

Ancient Rome, See Through History Series (Hamlyn Children's Books, 1992)

The Romans, History as Evidence Series (Kingfisher, 1992)

Rome and the Ancient World, Illustrated History of the World Series (Simon & Schuster, 1991)

Rome in the time of Augustus, Making History Series (Simon & Schuster, 1993)

The Roman Fort by P. Connolly (Oxford, 1991)

A Roman Villa, Inside Story Series (Simon & Schuster, 1992)

First published in 1976
by Usborne Publishing Ltd
Usborne House
83-85 Saffron Hill
London EC1N 8RT
England

Copyright © 1993, 1976 Usborne Publishing Ltd.

Printed in Belgium